Praise for *Only the Ocean*

'I was absolutely cheering on Kel and Rose by the end
of their stormy salt water odyssey! ... Wonderful,
mesmerising, immersive storytelling!'
Hilary McKay, award-winning author of
The Skylarks' War

'I loved *Only the Ocean*. It's about a girl who is trying
to escape from a dreadful life and an entire deck of
cards stacked against her ... It's about the new, hitherto
unimagined, escape routes that love can bring. This all
comes wrapped up in Carthew's singular and poetic style,
awareness of nature and use of dialect. I thought it was
wild and raw and truly, truly beautiful'
The Bookbag

'Steering clear of well-worn clichés, Carthew's
stories cut to the heart of human experience, often
portraying and championing life's underdogs and
outsiders. What a thrilling, thought-provoking novel
this is, brimming with perilous encounters, and the
rawness of real-life relationships'
LoveReading4Kids

'An intriguing LGBTQ story about survival and
fortitude, with a fierce protagonist at its heart'
Culturefly

'A vi‎   ‎vival,

Praise for *Winter Damage*

'Elegantly lyrical … A heart-rending quest story'
Susan Elkin, *Independent*

'A tough, heartbreaking story of loss, fear and friendship'
We Love This Book

'Small but perfectly formed, *Winter Damage* is the sort
of book that begs to be read out loud … A stone-cold
stunner with an uncommonly humble heart'
Niall Alexander, Tor

'A poetic, chilling and moving debut'
Love Reading

Praise for *The Light That Gets Lost*

'Wholly original … Carthew's language is enthralling'
Books for Keeps

'Poetic, with a magical and lyrical rhythm. Superb!
Highly recommended'
School Librarian

'A wild and dangerous story and a beautiful one too'
The Bookbag

'Carthew delivers a gripping story in intense,
powerful prose'
International Business Times

ONLY
The
OCEAN

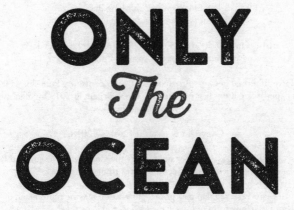

ONLY
The
OCEAN

NATASHA CARTHEW

BLOOMSBURY
LONDON   OXFORD   NEW YORK   NEW DELHI   SYDNEY

BLOOMSBURY YA
Bloomsbury Publishing Plc
50 Bedford Square, London WC1B 3DP, UK

BLOOMSBURY, BLOOMSBURY YA and the Diana logo
are trademarks of Bloomsbury Publishing Plc

First published in Great Britain in 2018 by Bloomsbury Publishing Plc
This paperback edition first published in Great Britain in 2019 by Bloomsbury
Publishing Plc

A catalogue record for this book is available from the British Library

ISBN: HB: 978-1-4088-6860-7; PB: 978-1-4088-6861-4;
eBook: 978-1-4088-6862-1

2 4 6 8 10 9 7 5 3 1

Typeset by RefineCatch Limited, Bungay, Suffolk

Printed and bound in Great Britain by CPI Group (UK) Ltd, Croydon CR0 4YY

To find out more about our authors and books visit www.bloomsbury.com
and sign up for our newsletters

For Evelyn

Chapter One

The decision to run from the shack was the right one and the only one available to the girl and she took it without a second thought.

She packed her bag and sheet-tied the baby to her back and she ran toward the gate, the gate that had been busted by looters and hung loose and merry in the wind.

The baby cried out with the sudden smack of cold and the girl reached around to slap it shut the same way Dad and the others always did. Maybe the girl knew it was wrong someplace inside but she had yet to learn another way.

She ran with her best-boots only-boots stabbing at the swamp-slop ground and lifted her legs high so as not to get pulled down into the muddy suck. If she could escape from the shack and the forest completely she would have a shot at the plan she had been working through.

When she was clear of the home track that slit the woods clean in half the girl paused for breath and she told the baby whether it was listening or not that they were heading down to the river town, because that was where she was meant to meet the man that had set the plan in motion. The man that came to the shack occasionally to buy goods had set her a task.

It was a plan that was meant for her and her alone; it had a name scribbled clean through it like a stick of rock and the name was Kel Crow and that was her name.

Kel stood at the edge of the woods where the canopy sheltered them a little and she took her raincoat from the bag and hooked it over both their heads. She looked at the stream below her that used to be a lane and she walked the bank above and kicked a clod of wet earth into it and in the end she closed her eyes and jumped across the body of water.

The other side of the stream used to be open farm land, or so they said. Kel could not remember a time before the floods and the constant rain that kept on coming whatever the time of year. These days the few crops still grown were planted in the disused gas drums that drifted above the ground. There was nothing left of the farm land but mud-sup plains; forever-fields of brown water, stagnant and still.

Kel stood a moment on top of a once-was wall. Her eyes walked its thin winding line in the direction of the town. The early morning sky was much like every other: heavy heaving clouds circling and spitting gumball lead that caught on the wind and fired furious like bullets. Seaward to the west of the town she could see the towers, the barred communities where the grand folk lived; mini societies where the air was filtered and luminous lights splashed into their domed skies like newly formed planets. In the minds of the swamp inhabitants the towers were another world entirely. Neither side mixed. Neither saw how the other half lived. Some days Kel wondered about them, but most days she didn't have the time, the energy. The towers were like mountains, distant.

When the baby cried out she took one of the biscuits she had been hoarding and stuck it into its mouth, and when she thought she might cry too with the effort of exertion and escape combined she stuck a biscuit into her own mouth the same.

If she could just get to town before anyone noticed she was gone, before Dad had time to realise the gate was still bust-broke and that the barbed wire had come down enough for the girl and the baby to get gone. If she could just walk the wall into town, keep her eyes away from the rising water and find the man who'd met her and liked her enough to hire her for the job.

Kel Crow was on her way and she felt like shouting out loud for all the hot-head scheming that was seared through it and so she picked up her feet, set a course along the rutted wall and started to run.

Kel entered the town as the boy who rang the bell for tips hung from his window to chime out twelve o'clock. She had been walking for three hours, if it wasn't for the risk of rot getting to her feet she could have gone on as far as forever. She untied the baby and put it to the ground in order to return life to her back and she stretched all ways to loosen the knots and bent to pick up the kid and she carried it in her arms through the plank-board streets whilst she observed her surroundings. The rivers and the streams and the memory of fields that once worked for something backalong were now linked one way or other with walkways and reclaimed pallets and planks and boats meant for stopping and idling: stepping stones precariously placed to make something of a community, no matter how unhinged.

To Kel community meant nothing more than disease and feuding and thieving and fearing just about. When people saw her they looked away because most knew Kel and her family. The Crows were drug-runners, pushers, the worst kind of swamper. Most had heard of the Crow girl with the wild streak running, she had danger in her eyes, same as her dad, and it was those eyes Kel fixed on the river bar, the one place on that sprawl of water-borne pontoons that passed for town where she knew the man was waiting for her.

Kel stood a minute outside the drifting, bumping clapperboard hut and she lit herself a cigarette to steady her nerves right for talking and when the baby griped at the smoke she blew more until its eyes closed tight.

The bar was a place of open any-old trade. People sat intent and pressed into each corner of the small stuffy room, men and women and youths like Kel who had grown wise with the work of a wretched life. Kel thinned her eyes to adjust to the smoky, candle-lit haze and she stood at the bar and asked to see the owner and said that he would be expecting her.

'One of em Crow kids, int you?' said the woman.

Kel shrugged the usual 'so what'.

'The girl, only Crow girl I heard of.' She looked at the baby. 'See you bin busy. I got some goods from you backalong for me old mother before she passed, came highly recommended.'

'Is that so?'

'I reckon.'

The woman told Kel to help herself to a beer whilst she went out back and Kel sat the baby in one of the half-barrel chairs and went behind the bar, poured herself a drink and then she waited.

She had waited her whole life for an opportunity such as this one. Fifteen years longing to escape. She wished it had come earlier, two years earlier, two years before the stupid me-me-me baby that never gave up on the whining and the crying out. She looked down at it and sighed and wondered why she had bothered to lug the thing along with her.

It bothered Kel that she might have weakness cracking within, but if she hadn't taken the baby its life would have become *her* life, lived all over again. Even a stupid baby didn't deserve that.

'You dodged a bullet,' she told it. 'I might not like you and you sure don't like me but I'm tellin you this is better un that cus that int no fun.'

'What int?' asked the man.

'Life,' said Kel, and she swung around on the stool to face the man standing behind the bar.

5

'You're right there.' He nodded and poured himself a beer and stretched close. 'So, you ready?'

'Born for it.' Kel stood tall. It was her way of showing how prepared she really was.

The man took a gulp of his pint, his eyes on Kel. She kept her eyes on him.

'So –' he set the glass down on to the bar – 'first things first, you remember the name of the ship you're meant for?'

Kel nodded. '*Kevothek.*'

'Remember what it means?'

'Cornish for "powerful".' She kicked at the sawdust on the floor and wondered if the man thought her stupid cus she wasn't.

'And the girl's name?'

'Rose. I also know to find her in the captain's quarters cus the captain sleeps in his office and she's his daughter.'

'And where's his office?'

'Bow room.'

The man smiled. 'That's it, he eats sleeps shits counts his money in there accordin to my source, calls himself a captain but em tower folk don't know nothin bout hard graft.'

Kel took a gulp of her beer and when she saw the baby looking she gave it a little on the tip of her thumb.

'And I told you it's a cargo ship?'

'Course.'

The man set down his beer and came around the bar. 'There's no room for error here, you know that, don't you? We all got somethin ridin on this.'

Kel nodded. If he only knew how much she had riding; it was the difference between life and death. 'I'll see you in three days at the docks, midnight, and you don't have to worry. I'll have the girl in tow.'

'And don't rough her up, I know what you Crows are like. Roughin up int part of the deal.'

'I int no animal,' said Kel and when the baby squealed she looked away. 'I bin over this a hundred times, I won't be seen, won't smack the girl, not even a hair. Three days and we'll be waitin for you at the gates, Falmouth docks.'

'And you sure you got a boat to get yourself down there?'

Kel nodded. That was the easy part.

The man smiled. 'OK then, Kel Crow gets a good job done, int that right?'

Kel shrugged a maybe but it was true. Nothing was too much for a girl with nothing to lose. Everything about the plan had brilliance carved into it and like a fairytale promise it was about to come true.

'I knew you were the one for the job.' He bent to pour them a whisky each; in the swamps a shot was as good as a promise and a handshake combined. 'Good for the job cus you're as strong as any lad I know but you got the cunnin of a girl, int I right?'

Kel nodded and she tried to agree but the whisky had its daggers in her throat.

'Strong as a boy and cunnin as a girl and twice over bein you're a Crow and all.'

Kel said yes and in her mind she knew she was good for the job on both accounts, but she had more driving force propelling her than that. The plan would lead to goods for keeping to herself, keeping and doing and selling as she pleased, and she put her hand to her heart to feel it beat out the irregular rhythm as always. She had always thought her heart would be the death of her, but now it was her life.

'You all right?' asked the man.

'More un.' She downed the whisky and the last of her beer and she told him she would never be anything other than all right again.

'Perfect,' he smiled. 'Perfect cus the *Kethovek*'s come in and it's about to back-turn.'

Kel nodded and she fingered the last tip of jar whisky and rubbed it on the baby's gums and then she tried her hand at smiling and said goodbye.

In three days Kel would have the first part of her plan completed. It seemed like forever had been planned and in a way it had, and she told the baby as they went to sit at the river edge that it had to be on its best behaviour, because this was it, this was the plan that would change their lives. If not, her heart was due to bust and break soon as, and if it did the baby would be good as dead the same.

Kel asked every bit-bob boat that came close enough for shouting to if they might be heading toward Falmouth Bay, but she knew she looked like trouble and that was fair enough because she just about was. She would have to go at things another way.

She sat back on the pontoon that was like every pontoon floating and settling beside the rivers in that part of Cornwall, and she watched the water run wild and rapid toward the sea beneath her swinging boots. No matter how much water fell from the leaden slate-pit sky it seemed there was always room for more in the dirt-crack fissures of the earth.

She wondered if there were other parts of the world worse than this sucking circle of landslides and rising tides and forever floods, and whether she might see some of that other world and not just dream about it. The floods were the worst; they washed and rubbed everything russet red with mud. They had split what they called civilisation in two. A fissure that had the swamp people grapple with the wash-away water whilst the rich slept high and happy in the clouds; clouds that circled the towers and surrounded them with trenches and walls the height of forever. Now Kel was that bit closer she could clearly see their beauty, the trees that circled the perimeters, the ivy that draped from the walls like curtains. She wondered what secrets they held.

She sighed and when the wind picked up and made waves in the river she unstuck the baby from off the tread-boards and stood to keep the wet from catching in her boots. She waited outside the bar and retied the baby. Then she climbed the ladder that clung for all its life was worth to the side of the river bed.

She spotted a speedboat that some fool had left ticking with the key still dangling and decided to steal it, even though she could see from its livery that the speedboat was also a law boat. If she could defeat the swamps and their death-rot squalor she could get to the coastline quickly and to the ocean that would lead to better things. She climbed aboard and strapped the baby in next to her best she could and she sat back against the hessian spring chair that had been skinned of its leather and with both hands tight to the steering wheel and her foot jammed to the floor she ran herself headlong speeding toward the south coast.

She gripped the wheel of the stolen boat with the whites of her knuckles flashing occasional red and she thought about her plan. She ran the details back and forward until it was set down clear as day. It was a good plan and more than that it was a doable plan; it had to be, because if it did not work she knew she would die.

Death in mind, this was how she negotiated the river; whooping and calling out to whoever-whatever that she was ocean bound and when the baby cried she whooped all the more to put happy into its ears. When at last the boat collided with the harbour wall of the docks she counted out her breathing, told her heart to quit with the run around, that it was made for action. Kel Crow, fierce on the outside when inside she was breaking bit by bit.

She put her hand to her chest and tallied back from ten. The heart was the start of it; born with a defect that made her fear for her life each day and then when the baby was born everyone said it was a done deal, game over. It was then that she first thought of escape, a last-ditch attempt at saving herself, all because of the stupid baby and her stupid heart that beat wrong and was shaped wrong and had wrongness stretched clean through it.

Kel grabbed her saddle bag, swaddled the baby and jumped from the boat. The solid ground felt good beneath her feet and she took a moment to glance at her surroundings. Evening light fanned dust shadows across the wet alleyways, and smoke from the boat's engine crept up the sides of buildings and caught beneath the gutters. Everything in slow motion, when all Kel could think of was speed.

She told herself to take a minute, stay hidden in the shadows and wait to see if anyone had noticed her or the police boat that was still smoking out on the water.

'OK,' she said to the baby, 'let's go,' and she tied it to her back and coiled her saddle bag around her neck.

Slowly she made her way toward the centre of the docks, the row of cargo ships jostling for space, their rigs and cranes so closely packed Kel couldn't see where one ended and the next began.

And all the while the sound of sirens getting nearer. They sounded like screams; it made her shudder, she'd never heard so many or so close, they rarely strayed far from the tower perimeters. Something was happening up ahead and instinct was to turn around, but Kel had come too far.

She was no longer alone, people stepped from the shadows and as they pushed past running in her direction she went with them. For these swamp people, to reach the ocean was to get to a boat and have half a chance of escaping from whatever this was. Perhaps it was a crime they had or hadn't committed, perhaps it was more than that.

Either way, Kel had never seen such mayhem. Something must've happened in the swamps. Kel had been so focused on her escape she hadn't given it heed, but now thinking back to town, the way folk looked at her and the way they looked at each other, there'd been something boiling beneath the surface, heat unnoticed.

There was always some kind of trouble brewing between the two sides, but this seemed different, worse, and whatever it was had the police armed and ready on the docks and the masses fearing and running for their lives. She wondered if the rich had prepared for this latest uprising, or if they even knew it was happening right beneath their feet. She doubted it.

Kel told the baby not to believe that there was no way out. That though they existed at the root of the rot and sat in the muck and the stench of the thing, still life went on, there were ways to make life go on. Kel didn't want what the tower people had; she wanted only two things, a heart she could rely on and freedom from kin.

As it was, the harbour and the docks in general had nothing to offer the screaming masses except the usual rough-neck looting trawlers and the cargo ships that ran guns and stolen goods back and forth across the Atlantic. Kel knew about the ships because she'd been thinking about them long before tonight. She reached into her boot and pulled out her note-book. The plan was set and firm, and she told the baby what it was she was meant to do in order to hear the plan out loud.

'Board the ship,' she whispered. 'Board the ship that's meant, then when out sailin merry in the ocean proper steal a dinghy and kidnap the girl.' She tilted her head to see if the baby was listening and it was. 'Now this is the best bit, swap the girl for the bag of goods and head out to Bottom America, then sell the drugs for the money that's gonna pay for the operation.'

She returned the notebook to her boot and smiled at the baby and told it to go back to sleep.

It had been her idea to ride out to South America for a long time now. Organs and operations were cheap out there, the only place for fixing up for a girl like Kel. She'd had the idea in place for forever, had read about the operations on a square of newspaper ripped for the loo, and it annoyed her now to have to find the ship the man had told her to board amongst so much panic. It was just her luck that today her running idea had become everyone's idea. She told the baby to hold on and she ran with the crowds a little, but Kel knew better than to straggle under the harbour lights. She could hear warning shots blast the night air, knew well not to ignore them. Soon the crowd would be dispersed and all folk gone back to idling, pleading with a god that did not exist. Kel was more than cynical; there had been a million scares and threats to the tower folk before and she'd concluded that fear for fear's sake was the culprit.

She ran on toward where she thought the ship would be, the vessel that would bring her safely to a new life, her destiny. The one-two-three fortune story that went: get the girl, swap for drugs, sell the drugs to pay for the operation. She went over it again and again like a chant. One-two-three and her life would start over again. A new life in a new country with a partway new kind of heart, fixed and ready for whatever. And it didn't matter what stage of chaos the new country was in because it wasn't *this* one and more importantly it wasn't her chaos.

She circled the docks and filtered out through the crowd and onward toward where she knew the cargo ships were moored. When she reached the clapperboard warehouses she found a cubby of tarred, useless nets and settled herself to watching and waiting. How many ships? It was hard to tell; she counted eight – nine maybe – each one pushed against the next, stacked with steel crates and what names she could see she said out loud but it didn't help. Where was her ship, where was the *Kevothek*?

'Shit.' Kel stood up and climbed the dune of nets. Somewhere out there was her ship, it had to be; she had not planned for anything other than victory. One more scan of the horizon, one last-ditch attempt to find something of meaning …

It was then that she saw it; a flag in tatters, but its name was unmistakeable.

'The *Kevothek*.'

The black of dark and acrid smoke combined shielded Kel from the clutch of watchful deckhands and she watched the armed guards patrol the ship. She observed where they stood and counted out the time between each one's circuit as she double-tied the baby tight to her back. The third man to come round walking the third time had the longest space tailing him. He walked too fast and the man behind walked too slow and into that timeless void Kel ran and jumped with the bag and the baby strapped and saddled wrong and she hit the deck with a crack.

Chapter Two

Kel lay on her front and waited for her something to start hurting. When nothing did she reached around to check the baby, clubbed a hand to its mouth and listened for the wet slap skid of running footsteps, and when none came she pushed herself fully beneath the hot beating purr of stirring engines. She slowed her breathing down to an easy-draw beat and waited for her heart to fall in the same and then she furthered back between the huge metal crates that towered all around and there she paused for thinking time.

She could hear gunfire, a warning shot, and the screams of people running-rabbit at the main harbour side a few hundred metres back. She imagined their footsteps slipping on the wet ground, getting closer to the *Kethovek*, and she prayed the ship set sail before they had a chance to get down to this end of the harbour. Kel knew the chaos would not end tonight; it never did. She untied the baby and lay in the snuggle-warm with it lying near to her and when survival instinct returned she sat up.

A bit of fresh salt air was blowing, waking her and Kel was happy to sit up and wait. She'd wait for evening shadows to pull the cargo containers snug around her and when night came fully she'd think over the next stage of her plan and she would think it over good.

She wasn't just running for the sake of freedom: she was heading toward a future set out in perfect star formation and she couldn't wait to get fixed up, have a pin put in her heart or whatever it was to bring its size back down to normal. Some fool-folk reckoned it was a good thing to have a big heart; it wasn't.

With good thoughts settling she lay back on her bursting saddle bag that housed all and everything she had in the world, and she turned it buckle down so there was some comfort for her head within the dip of material. She watched as a drift of ripped black-sack clouds crept across the thin wedge of sky above. Their silent wandering had Kel float out in her own mind and she closed her eyes to enjoy sudden solitude, even made something of cuddling the baby. Kel could hear the curl of ocean as it licked and sucked at the ship's hull and the slow clink of chain as it retreated and pulled the anchor free of water. She imagined the lift of each of the other vessels' bulging bellies as the sea caressed them with tender hands, the beckoning mystery of foreign lands whetting their appetite for the unknown, along with that of every man and runaway and crazy that stood onboard their decks.

Kel had no such appetite. She only wanted what should have been hers; health and a simple life just being. Adventure was not for her. There were enough wilds in her as it was; enough of the unknown to declare herself uncharted, a stand-alone live-alone island, a rock, no matter how she crumbled inside.

She pulled the baby close.

The last of daylight slid by unnoticed. Bit by bit the sky dipped dark and grew void of colour, nothing but the mix-black palette of midnight in the middle of nowhere. Kel listened out for the constant burp and banter of harbour seagulls but there was none. All she heard was the whirr of engines punching and clocking up speed. The ship was finally moving. She sat up and pulled her denim jacket from the bag and wrapped it about her shoulders and she tucked the bed-blanket and the raincoat around the baby to keep it from rolling and she scanned the sky in the hope of star camaraderie, but the black night gave nothing away.

She looked down at the sleeping kid; it was the worst kind of companion. 'You better be on your best behaviour,' she said and she shoved it into hiding and stood to stretch the cold deck floor from her bones. She had work to exact, no time to lose. Everything was in place.

The first thing on her list was to locate the girl, it wouldn't be hard. There was no other girl on the ship besides herself. Rose would be a flower amongst thorns, a sore thumb sticking out. Kel would sneak around under cover of darkness until she'd pinpointed the girl and sourced a lifeboat. Then Kel and the baby would need somewhere safer to hide and wait, ready for when the time was right for kidnapping. In Kel's mind it was as pure as quartz; it held all the light she needed to see it clearly.

She set off following the maze of storage crates that stretched wall-high and were everywhere about the ship. Kel could tell they were heading down the English Channel; the thin leaving light on that scoop-curve of horizon port side told her so. The faint wash of pink and orange hues leaked into the forever ocean like a snaking oil slick, spoiling the black ink with its rainbow spillage.

Kel stepped into her new world with all the command she thought was in her possession. The ship and its thump-and-threat din and the firm grip of deck beneath her feet were a million miles from home and it was perfect.

She looked around at her surroundings and was careful not to step too far from the shadows, told herself that no matter what she would keep to the plan. Two nights to make sure the ship was away and heading, two nights to keep the head down and the eyes watching; see the girl, get the girl and get gone.

There were plenty of people onboard ship with heeding ears, not just everyday people but strangers and stragglers and plain old crazies, working the ship for cash because they were all out of chances on the mainland. Men who couldn't get work or a life that fitted right would hit the high seas with a two-bit coin between their teeth and a little hope in their hearts. Kel knew about that kind of hope, she had it big and ballooning in her chest just the same.

She leaned to the railings and peered down toward the waves that lifted the hull and she looked at the diminishing lights of Falmouth and raised a hand goodbye, told it to wait for her cus in two days she would return, she promised it this.

Kel said goodbye to the flickering candy town for the sake of maudlin and moved on from the railings so she could see something more of the ship. If the plan was going to work she had to know its gangways, the secret tunnels and the rough-neck workers who inhabited the oily spent place. She would watch their every move and fill the idling gaps between with her movement, keep a hundred steps ahead to keep from being discovered. She followed the starboard railings that penned the edge of the ship and was careful not to slip on the greasy deck. Tonight she would find the captain's quarters and see the girl to stamp the last detail of the plan into being.

She kept to the thin elevated shadows and turned her ear from the noise of the smash-and-grab waves and the constant clank of gearing engines and she made sure to be nothing to the men but empty space.

Suddenly she heard a shout somewhere on the upper deck. A fight was breaking out, she knew the sound all too well. She climbed the steel ladder that clung to the side of the quarterdeck and was careful with the footing, and when she reached the top she hooked her arms between the metal bars and wedged herself against the warm purr of a generator and this was where she saw them properly for the first time.

Men and boys were jostling for space out on the deck. They pushed and shoved back against each other until a circle was formed around two fighters and Kel turned and wiggled into position so she too could watch the battle, even though she knew not to expect to see the girl there. She was a prim-posh tower girl; a kid like that wouldn't understand the primal need to fight.

Kel ducked each time eyes idled her way and she bit down on the nerve that wanted to run so she could see the victor suck up the win, taste the sugary-sharp brilliance that violence brought. Kel knew about blood and bone and the beat that exposed both and she wondered why anyone would want to fight for anything other than survival. Not that it mattered; their stupidity was her gain. It would give her the chance to explore the ship while they watched the blood get sluiced from the deck and they fixed their eyes on the next two men and turned their minds to the placing of new bets.

Kel took her time to walk the length of the vessel toward the captain's quarters. She guessed it was at the front tucked out of the way.

'Somewhere quiet,' she told herself, 'somewhere hidden.'

She reached the bow and saw the last remaining feature on the ship: a small hut-like structure studded to the deck and the sign on the door read 'Captain's Mess' so this was the place.

Kel stood close to the door and held her breath. She hadn't expected to find it so easily, she needed time to work out what she was doing. She felt for her notebook in the back pocket of her jeans for reassurance.

'Just a recce,' she whispered. 'See the girl to know that she exists.'

Kel told herself to think of her as the enemy, or, even easier than that, cargo. The girl was just goods after all, a component in a long line of workings that joined together, would fill all four corners of her beautiful, faultless plan.

She put her nose to the window and squinted to see if she could see light and turned her ear for noise, but nothing. Maybe the girl was asleep. She'd heard that tower kids were lazy, useless. Kel reached for the handle and found it gone but in its place a key. She unlocked the door and went in.

Two rooms, one for sitting and one for lying down. Kel knew the girl was not here, of course not, the door had been locked from the outside and there was not one sign of anybody at all, no sign that any girl had ever been there.

Kel left the cabin the way she found it and decided to head below deck; if the girl wasn't here perhaps a room had been made up for her down there. Since the menfolk were above deck then not many would be below and Kel acknowledged the situation as a chance to plunder food whilst she looked for the girl.

She retraced her footsteps and saw that the men had settled to other entertainments: a wooden chest upturned, a pack of cards produced. Men and boys all cut the same took their places around the makeshift table, some with money some without; they circled the action, roped around three times like a noose. Cards were dealt and matchsticks counted out for that'll-do chips, and when all heads dipped to the silence of the ocean's push and pull Kel crept fully toward deck and she tiptoed from one shadow to the next until she found the hole that led down toward the main living quarters and she put her boot to the first rung of the ladder and climbed down.

Below deck the drill of engines turning over seeped into every corner of the ship. Every vent and pipe, every wooden crate rattled with the sound of movement, a floating gun-laden death ship bound for unfamiliar things on the forever sea. Kel bent to one of the crates and wondered what they were carrying. The sign said Food, Kitchen, but the way the contents knocked together sounded all wrong for tins and supplies. She stood back. The first time she met the man at the river bar he told her not to wonder what the ship was carrying, but when pushed he told her it was guns looted from the naval base in Plymouth and at the time Kel had thought them stupid: drugs were one thing, but guns were another, they were instant, bang-bang, game over. Kel'd bet anything that the contents of these crates were weapons.

She hurried through the squash-gut gangways with the fluorescent lights that flashed on and off and kept her nose in the air, but if there was food cooking Kel couldn't smell it for the thick tang retch of oil and diesel that was everywhere.

She went on looking and listened out for anything other than grinding cogs and when she stumbled across the dining mess she took a minute to assess her surroundings, the jumble of empty cups and plates, and she didn't worry about what it was to be a girl if she was discovered standing there because she was a big bully-boy type of girl. Kel took to rooting and was quick to find bread half ripped and a slab of cheese just sitting and she took off her jacket and bundled them into it and grabbed a carton of milk from the cooler and she stuffed the lot beneath her arm. If there were other things worthy of the steal she would have taken them but what was left of a meal was bit and spilled and smeared, and Kel was happy with her plunder and happier still to be close to eating it. She hadn't eaten much in recent days and she could feel the brittle snap of frailty in each and every bone.

She left the room and traced her way back through the narrow muddle-maze and up to the deck. Maybe it was the spin of giddy-greed hunger that had her mind single-tracked but she went at a pace about the ship and she forgot to mind herself completely.

As Kel made her way back to her little hideout amongst the crates she imagined the food sandwiched and stuffed and the milk swilled to dregs and her mouth juiced with hunger.

At times she heard laughter jab the surrounding night air. The men's whereabouts confused her, made her jump, the milk slipped and wasted. 'Shit.'

She lay on her chest and wriggled beneath the metal pipes that tangled and spiralled across the upper deck.

She stuck close to the ground and pulled the food close, her eyes following the stud-line of rivets that pushed against her cheek until she found the ladder. She pressed her ear to the stick-grit floor to listen for shouts and the thud-thud of catching footsteps but there were none.

Kel found the baby and struggled further beneath the hot turning machines, she wished she hadn't dropped the carton of milk she had been looking forward to it, now all that was left was dry bread and cheese, wet clothes. She rolled the bit of food between her fingers and chewed and swallowed over: the cheese tasted of salt and the bread tasted of nothing at all. The stodge mopped moisture from her mouth and it fisted and forced its way into her chest with a punch.

Kel could hear the engines step up gear and she knew they were running at full speed now, she could feel the vibrations in every bone and her stomach buzzed with loose fitting. For all her Cornish blood she hated the sea. To see the ocean was one thing, its moated border meant protection and security, but to be on it was another thing entirely, it meant danger and at high speed double danger.

She pushed the remaining food into the space behind the baby and closed her eyes and blocked her ears partway to the ratatat but the shake was in her and she could feel the rise from her gut to her throat. She slide from her hideout and ran to the railings with the sick racing from her. In one brief moment nothing else mattered but the purge; to have her belly sucked clean down deep within the coop of riding rib-bone.

Kel lent into the railings and doubled over with the retch and she hung in weary desperation until serenity returned. She breathed the wet sea spray and pulled it into her lungs and it was a blast of smelling salts. Her stomach unclenched and she spat the bitter from her mouth and wiped with her sleeve and she wished again for something more than nothing to quench her thirst.

The night had come in fast and with it a mist as thick as netting cloth and Kel could feel the damp curl her hair and take what dry there was from out her clothes. She stared into the roiling dark and it tangled her and caught her where she stood and there was so much of the spin about her that she felt less of herself than what was usual. She looked beyond the ocean to where the lights of land had been and lifted the collar of her jacket. She pulled up her sleeve and her left hand felt for the self–inflicted scars on her arm and she took comfort in them. The ridges lay like tracks and were etched deep into the skin and each one told a story of the spirit that was in her.

It was a journey that ran up and down her arm like a runaway carriage, crashing and burning and crashing again. Kel's life was a trainwreck, a tangle of metal and detritus that indicated a life lived far from civilisation. The lines on her arm were mapped for a reason, if only she could read them, understand what they told her in regards to where she had been and where she was heading. She looked again toward the cloak of mist that had thickened to rain and closed her eyes to let the water wash her clean, one moment of calm to wish it beneath her skin and cleanse her soul the same.

Kel went to check that the baby was breathing after so much quiet and it was. She fed it with her own milk and changed it and returned it to the warm snug hole and she lay down beside it and her mind settled on the girl and Kel thought about her long into the night.

She wondered about the journey that awaited them, some kind of fate tying them together in the secret knowledge that they both existed somewhere on the ship. Where was the girl, she had to be someplace. Kel had no other plot, no other way of thinking.

When sleep finally came it was the kind without dreams. The dark night seeped into her pores and settled just below the skin. A thin layer of dark matter, of misery and despair that tried to take her, turn her. Kel pulled her jacket tight to stuff the gaps with body warmth and she blocked out the dreamless night with optimism. Without optimism life wasn't worth much more than standing in line and sitting out time and lying and waiting to die.

Soon the girl would be swapped for drugs without her kin knowing what or when and they'd be back out on the ocean soon as. Kel only hoped whatever was happening on the mainland had finished happening by the time they got back. This was the positive drill that bore down in her when she lay to sleep and that was how she remained until morning.

Chapter Three

Kel rolled on to her back and she winced with the pain that lying without bounce had inflicted. She saw the dark smack of an anvil cloud hammering above. It meant another storm day coming: she felt a little of the wet curdling and threatening on the wind. She sat up and stretched and checked the baby for life and went to stand at the railings to listen to the rhythm of morning work.

She stepped into the alley that ran between two containers and crouched to a small puddle that had formed in the ship's beaten metal floor and she bent to it and sucked a little of last night's rain for thirst and splashed her face to freshen. To put something of normality into life was to have something of a normal life return.

Kel knew this was the time to prepare for the days ahead, go over what she had to do; kidnap the girl, launch a lifeboat and leave as quickly as possible.

She sat away from the baby and leaned close to the alleys

and creases of space that framed each of the toppling cargo crates and she thought about what comfort they might contain other than guns, the everyday things used to mask the truth. Perhaps one or two of the crates hid a bundle of domestic delight; soft furnishings and homelies to find and fiddle, a place to sleep and a place to huddle for the next night only night before the strike.

She stood and counted out the cargo crates and there were many. She tallied them into the sky and they ran five above, five high and a hundred long. The ship was huge. She wondered how big; she only knew miles, guessed it was at least half a mile in length. She tried to guess how long it would take to escape once she had the girl; she planned for hours, hoped for minutes, the quicker the better. She was glad of the orange rubber dinghy that hung at the edge of the ship. She told herself to keep it close and marked it as hers for the next part of her journey.

Kel took her time to move amongst the crates like a cat.

She looked for every possible place and rattled as many as she could but found none open nor bust. There was no alternative, she would have to break in and so she returned to the baby and fed it and she tied it to her back and told it to not make a sound because they were going to climb the crates. If she could find a corner of quiet away from the ship's hub she could wait out the twenty-four hours in relative comfort and with that one good thought she went to the bow where the crates were highest and she climbed the first ladder and then the next and negotiated the ledges until she could go no further. 'This'll do just fine,' she said to the baby and she told it to hold tight whilst she took her knife from the scabbard and picked the lock and slid the door wide.

Inside the crate Kel rolled the baby to the floor and she looked in every corner of the damp box but there was nothing but dust for kicking. Hours came and went, and Kel did all she could to shape the redundant time into a routine of getting up and lying down and keeping watch between. She knew she had to dig deeper into the ship's belly in order to find the girl.

She was careful to keep the baby bundled and hidden in the corner of the crate. and as the hours passed her by she continued to feed it when it asked for milk and change it when it cried discomfort and she washed the towel rags she used for its nappies in the everywhere puddles and she would tell it to shut up when it plain old yelled for nothing but attention. It was a stupid baby, if it wasn't it would have put its fist to its mouth and left it there for gumming. When it screamed and was fed and returned to screaming, Kel fought the compulsion to heave the crate door open and sling it to the wilds. On those occasions she told herself that would have been time wasted since she'd brought it this far, and she supposed it was wrong in any case. Finally she gave in to petting the baby and she lay it on her stomach and their breathing drifted and pooled complete and this was how they slept and they would have slept the journey through if it wasn't for the baby waking her up.

The day had been and gone and a new night heavy with

low-lying fog had arrived without warning and it sat poised, ready for command. Kel sat up and pushed the baby from her and she stretched to find her bag in the dark in order to get the candle she had been carrying and she lit it with her lighter and dripped wax to stick it to the floor and she stood and went to look out of the door. The night pushed on with the stop-start stretch of struggling engines and the dissonance kept Kel awake, she was sick of waiting, she knew the time for action was close.

She stood and pushed the door wide and looked toward the ship's deck, imagined Rose standing down there. Kel told herself the girl belonged to her, she needed to pinpoint for certain where she was. To have her close was to imagine the thing that had to be done, the grab and snatch that was the beginning of all things turning right. Kel could feel it in the moving marrow of her bones, a small clock ticking, telling her it was almost time.

The decision to look for her now was vital. Despite Kel knowing there was danger in being spotted, she had to place the girl in order to have her set right for the snatch and grab. She wasted no time in pushing the baby into hiding along with her miserly belongings and she checked her knife for the sharp ping-ping and it was good for doing and good for threatening if that was where things were heading.

Beneath the dull weight of darkness Kel shut the metal two-door on her secret life and climbed from the crate and she wound her way through the narrow tin-alley streets until she found the ladder that led to the upper deck.

31

There was something in the air that stuffed up the night wind and was wet-backed like rain, but the rain had long gone since. This was a creep and a crawl type thing that smelt of decomposition.

She climbed down the ladder and slid on to the deck with her eyes scooting every which way. She could smell the stench of unwashed men and the clog and dribble of a billion cigarette butts and beer cans thrown and they were everywhere. She toed the deck with her big boots shuffling for the quiet and looked out for clues to the girl's whereabouts, whilst the splash of wet that had her feet sticking nothing more to her than hindrance until she bent to it. She put one finger to the stick and held it up to the swing of light that came and went with the swim of ship and she saw the red and knew there had been another fight. The men had had a night of it and had tasted blood and maybe they were out for more. This was how things went in their world and Kel knew this because it was the same in hers. Maybe a fight had got out of hand, a fight with two halves to it or a fight between many. It didn't matter, the girl was still missing. Kel stood steady as a moment of quick-flash fear crept over her. What if the girl was not onboard ship at all. What then?

Maybe she was making too much of it. She had to find the girl, had to find her to know that she and the plan existed. Life sucked and double sucked for the sake of living. She stuffed her hands into her pockets and ran to the hatch that led below board and she put an ear and nothing came back and she stepped forward and turned both ears to listening.

Deep down within the body of the vessel she could hear some style of serious talk and she went forward and crouched in the odd green light and waited. Some words travelled toward her like a gift but most were mere mumbling lines of not much. Kel closed her eyes and tried to connect the dots. When she heard the girl's name she jumped. It felt funny hearing it out loud for some reason; the name Rose belonged to her. Down there somewhere buried in the bowels of the ship the name Rose was being passed around and it reminded Kel of home, of the way the men talked about her. Kel's heart beat faster thinking about it, the girl's potential danger felt like her own.

She stood back, the fighter in her falling and she wanted to flee, escape all over again. The voices were getting louder now, and Kel realised suddenly that two men were standing at the bottom of the ladder. Her instinct was to run, put this night to bed, but what if the girl really was in danger? She took a deep breath and crouched at the side of the hatch to listen.

'Good lookin maid,' said a voice. 'If I was younger and all that.'

'Surprised that would stop you, if this Rose girl is up for it and all. Seems like a right party girl.'

They both laughed and Kel gripped the top rung of the ladder in anger.

'Bit posh for a stowaway though, int she?' the second man continued.

'Who cares? All girls are the same with a bit of drink in em.'

33

Kel heard the clink of bottles being pulled from storage and the voices fade toward the music and she stood. Rose was a name that would keep spiking the stoic night, it was a source of laughter both fierce and threatening.

Kel took her knife from the scabbard and she held it close pressed to the salt-dry denim of her jacket. There was nothing for it but to descend into the hot hell searing beneath, a hell that stank of beef-fat frying and toilets that had long lost the flush. Kel sensed a secret lived down there amongst the men, a secret that had them merry and bashful and hardly able to keep fingered to their lips. Something exciting and something wrong and like idiots they laughed it all the way from bad to quite funny after all. This was how Kel read it. She descended further into the heat and stench and she thought things through best she could and the facts gleaned she laid out before her like tiny rip-clipped pieces of paper and everything spelt wrong. In her mind something had happened and by the cloying air filled with whispers Kel reckoned it was something bad. Something bad but to the men it was also something funny, something they couldn't help for the fact that it happened and by the nature of the thing it wasn't their fault.

Kel leaned into a shadow that came to her like a cool wash cloud between two lights and the thoughts that splintered inside her came together and stuck bone to nerve in the making of it. She moved between the dark places and her head reeled with the sound of monotony music and the notion of what might be happening.

In that moment something strengthened and broke inside, the recollection of the shack in the woods and of fear with all the tearing and biting still in it. Suddenly Kel ran wild with anger, the plan that she had taken so long to construct gone complete. She ran into open cabins with her knife flashing red-light warning and when she reached the room of voices and bad music she slowed, stopped to look through the crack in the door.

Kel returned her knife to the scabbard and stood with her back against the wall and put her hand to her chest and pleaded with her heart to please god be good. She waited for her breathing to slow and then she turned her head to the party.

At first it was hard to see much more than the men. They were all kinds of drunk: some laughing, some lurching, others were arguing toward a fight. She wondered if she had imagined the girl, was about to turn back when she heard it. Singing. Kel closed her eyes to let the moment wash over her, how could so much beauty exist in a place like that?

Kel looked up suddenly and that was when she saw her. 'Rose,' she whispered.

A part of her knew this was a bad idea, of course it was. The plan was to kidnap the girl without being seen, steal her away without anyone ever knowing she had come and gone again. She leaned against the wall so she could see clearer, watched the men group into a circle and caught glimpses of the flash of pink amongst them – the girl was singing, laughing, she danced amongst the men like a puppet. She didn't care what happened to her she was that flying drunk.

Kel didn't know what to do. She looked back down the corridor from where she had come, turned to leave, her heart in her mouth and her head telling her to calm down, but there was something about the girl, that voice, and before she knew it the knife had returned to her hand and Kel to the door.

The men saw her like a rapturous apparition as they spun drunk and falling, and she pushed and kicked and called out that she was here for the girl.

Kel looked about the room and called out to Rose, it was as if it were she herself who needed rescuing, like she was returning herself to the scene of a crime two years too late.

She looked around at the shocked faces, saw the girl hiding drunk in the corner of a nothing-much cabin and she pulled at her and dragged her from the room. Men came at Kel drunk and wary and some had a go at pinning her to the wall but each time she flashed her knife and managed to pull free.

Some of the men still laughed as they gave chase.

'Two girls! All the more for sharin!' she heard somebody shout.

Kel hated that. The knife twitched against the palm of her hand as she stopped and turned. 'What makes you think you can treat girls this way?' she shouted. 'Who gave you the goddamn right?' She held out the knife and realised she was shaking. 'Get behind me!' she told the girl.

The men stopped in their tracks.

'Well?' she asked them.

One of the older men stepped forward. 'Give us back the girl.'

Kel shook her head. 'She int yours.'

'Int yours either,' he said.

'Hello?' Rose put up her hand. 'Do I get a say?'

'We'll find you,' the man continued. 'This is a ship, if you int noticed.'

'Oh I noticed,' said Kel, 'I notice everythin. Now stay back.'

Kel stabbed the knife toward them and she ran fast with the girl clutched to her and she didn't stop until the men were tangled in confusion amongst the tower-high crates, their anger turning to laughter because what did they care?

Under cover of the black nothing night she put the knife to the girl so they might climb toward the room of nothing but dirt and rattling space. She was hers now, safely so.

'Who are you?' shouted the girl. 'What the hell do you think you're doing?'

'Keep goin,' Kel shouted. 'All the way inside.'

She made the girl go to the corner of the room and she bent to light the candle and she pulled the door shut. She stood and watched her take her bearings a moment.

'They was hurtin you,' said Kel, finally.

'They were?' asked the girl.

'They was gunna. I heard em talk.'

'About what, what are you talking about?'

'You, what they'd done, what they was bout to do.' Kel rubbed her head, it was heavy with thought. Things changed, she knew this, but the shipmates knowing about her existence, she could have done without that. She wasn't meant to capture the girl until the morning.

She looked out across the ocean, were they far enough out? Kel didn't think so, they would have to wait out the night.

'Damn.' She looked over at the girl and noticed she was laughing, mocking her, and Kel's hands filled with punch.

'So you're a stowaway?' the girl asked.

Kel watched Rose pull a half-drunk bottle of whisky from her jacket pocket. 'No,' she said.

'Of course you are, why, do you think you're the first? There's no use in pretending. Jesus, I'm one too.' Rose smiled, she seemed to be enjoying the attention. 'Even my dad doesn't know I'm here, this ship is no place for a girl.' She looked Kel up and down. 'No matter what you look like.'

'So your dad doesn't know you're onboard ship?' Kel asked.

'It'd kind of take the fun out of being a stowaway if he did.'

Kel thought about this, it all made sense, why the girl had been so hard to find.

'I guess em blokes wouldn't have tried it on with you if they knew whose kid you was.'

'Hey, who are you calling a kid?'

Kel ignored the girl, she told herself things were still on track, better even; nobody knew the captain's daughter was on the ship and as far as the men were concerned she was just some stowaway same as Kel, just posher and prettier. Tomorrow they would be busy nursing their hangovers and when thought returned to the two girls, Kel and Rose would be long gone.

She looked at the girl and realised she was still talking.

'I'm talking to you.'

'What?' asked Kel.

'I asked who you were calling a kid?'

Kel didn't know what to say so she didn't say anything, she hadn't reckoned on the girl being a big mouth, that wasn't part of the plan. She moved from the door to check the baby and she pushed it aside so she could sit on the blanket.

'Don't move,' she whispered to Rose. 'Don't move and sit down.'

'Why?' She grinned. 'Are you planning to slit my throat otherwise?'

'Yes.' Kel looked at the girl to see if she understood the things she herself knew as fact, but her smugness indicated she was far from understanding, 'And you better keep your voice down, better shut it or …'

'What?'

'Else.' Kel looked at the bottle in the girl's hand and told her to roll it over and the girl did and Kel took a long swig.

'So?' asked the girl.

'What?'

'Are you going to kill me or did you just save me? I'm confused.'

'Shut up.' Kel lit herself a cigarette and sat back.

'You got one of those for me?'

'Nope.'

'I gave you some of my whisky.'

Kel took a cigarette from the pack and lit it off her own and she flicked it into the girl's lap.

'Charming.'

Kel ignored her and went to stand at the open door and then she sat with her legs dangling and she told the girl to come sit the same.

'Don't push me.' The girl laughed.

'If I wanted you dead I would have left you to them men.'

'I was just making friends. I didn't ask to be saved or whatever the hell this is.'

Kel looked at Rose to see if she was funning the way shack menfolk did, but the girl wasn't and she returned her gaze to sea, from where they sat stern high above the waves, they could have gone unnoticed forever.

Light from the pared moon gave them something for seeing by and Kel looked at the thunderhead clouds as they jostled for space above the ocean floor. Big banging bags of rain the weight of spanners that would soon clash and send sparks flying. She turned to watch the girl drink some of the whisky then took it from her and did the same.

'I hope you're not planning on sucking that thing gone,' said the girl. 'It is mine.'

'Mine now.'

'Actually it's my dad's.' The girl looked at Kel and told her she was strange and Kel said she knew that already.

'Not going to tell me your name?' the girl asked. 'At least then I'll know who's doing the killing or whatever this is.'

'Keryn,' said Kel, 'Kel for short.' She looked at the girl and told her she was not going to kill her.

'My name's Rosen, but everyone calls me Rose.'

They sat in silence with the bottle passing between them and watched the clouds rebound out on the horizon and Kel knew it wouldn't be long before they chased the sky down and ended up duelling above their heads.

'It's a nice night,' said the girl suddenly, 'either way.'

'What?' asked Kel.

'The night, it's beautiful.'

Kel looked at the girl and then she looked at the clouds that were hurtling towards the ship. It was starting to rain. 'It's a storm,' she said.

'Lovely though isn't it? Lovely and beautiful and sad all mixed up the same.'

Kel shrugged. The girl was like nobody she had ever met, she looked at the world from some skewed angle, melancholy for the sake of twisted pleasure. Rich-kid bored-kid thoughts.

'It's just a storm,' Kel said again. 'I don't like storms.' She looked at Rose and said she'd seen trees rubbed out to nothing but ash on the ground because of lightning.

'I doubt it.'

Kel nodded. 'Seen a church steeple explode to flyin dust the same, don't you see no storms in them towers you live?'

'How do you know I live in the towers?'

41

'Cus duh.'

'The towers are mostly covered for protection, we only go out when the sun shines.'

'That int so often.' Kel looked across at the girl and told her she wasn't what a stowaway looked like.

Rose laughed. It made a ridiculous sound. 'You are.'

Kel looked away.

'I suppose you're wondering?' the girl went on.

'What?' asked Kel.

'Why I stowed away on my own father's ship.'

Kel shrugged. She didn't care, all she knew was the girl was meant for her plan to work.

'Boredom,' said the girl. 'Isn't that terrible? I was bored.'

'You bored now?'

'To be honest I am a bit, I was having a ball with the lads, until you came along.'

Kel took out her knife and pretended to clean her nails for the scare but it didn't work.

'If you knew the towers you would know what I mean.'

Kel returned her knife to the scabbard.

'I wish for adventure,' the girl continued.

Kel wished for silence, a few minutes would have been something, the posh girl would not shut up.

When the rain slashed at their swinging legs they went inside and Kel told the girl that she they would not be leaving the container tonight. 'You can lie down beside the baby,' she told her.

'Do I get a choice?' asked Rose.

'What you reckon?' Kel stood at the door and finished the bottle and she listened to the thundering clouds and watched the lightning come close and hitting, and she didn't close the doors and would not bed down until the storm had passed fully.

When finally it did she sat at the corner of the blanket and watched the girl fumble with a new cigarette she'd taken from Kel's pack, and when she fell asleep with the dumb-drunk punch of too much drink Kel leaned forward and took the cigarette into her own mouth and she smoked it down to her fingers and lay down the same.

When dawn arrived they would be far enough from land that the plan could be put into play: a little light in which to navigate, set the dinghy to water and return to the mainland.

All night through Kel idled with her ears stretched open to night noises so when morning came she had been waiting for it. It brought no change to her world except a thin slip of surprise sunlight that pried open the heavy metal doors and settled at Kel's feet. She leaned forward to watch it sparkle and smile and there was something in that ray of light that had promise dusted into it. In the bit of light she bent to her to check that the girl was alive the same way she did each day for the baby.

'I'm not dead,' said the girl.

'I know, just checkin.' Kel couldn't have this kidnap thing go wrong, it was time to get the job done proper and get off the ship for good. She watched the baby wake and when it started to beg she picked it up and turned her back to the girl

43

so she could feed it and when the baby was stuffed enough she returned to the door.

'What are you going to do?' asked Rose.

Kel ignored her.

'Maybe you should start praying, Stowaway, if you're god-fearing. Some of you swampers are, aren't you?'

'I int,' said Kel flatly.

'Well maybe you should be, maybe *I* should. Perhaps that's my problem.'

Kel opened the two-door just a little and peeked out.

'Anything?' asked Rose. 'I should go and tell Dad I'm OK.'

'I thought you was a stowaway too?'

'I am, but the lads would have told him about you and if they said about you they would have said about me.'

'That int fact,' said Kel.

'What's that?'

'They dint come lookin, did they, last night.'

'How do you know what they did and didn't do?'

'They was drunk for one and two they didn't tell your dad you was a stowaway and three …'

'Yes and three? I'm waiting.'

'Shush, be quiet.'

'Well I'm ready to go, thank you for saving me from whatever you thought I needed saving from and, of course, the witty conversation, but I really have to go.'

'You can't.'

'I think you'll find I can.'

Kel hung from the door, it was time to move, now. She was

prepared for two things only, settle the lifeboat to water then return for the girl, a few minutes was all it would take. She told the girl to be quiet and put on her jacket and swung her bag crossways against her back.

'Where are you going?' Rose shouted but Kel ignored her. 'What about the baby?'

'Sing to it.'

'I only like pop songs.'

'Sing them.'

'Thought you told me to be quiet?'

Kel stepped out on to the top rung of the ladder. 'No shoutin, just. You're a stowaway, remember?'

She pushed the door closed and tied the outside chain into a knot, there was no way the girl was getting out of there until Kel returned.

She climbed down the turret of crates with her knife flashing ready in one hand and her notebook in the other. She was prepared for two things only: settle the lifeboat to water then return for the girl.

She sidled past one crate and the next and the next until she reached the gangway that would lead her to the steps below deck. The orange boat that had been there yesterday would be there today, she only wished she had the time to fill it with food.

She tapped her knife to the railings and she rolled the glint of surprise sunlight across its blade like a solitary tear. She would get the boat and the girl and get off the stupid ship immediately.

She stood with her hands on the railings and looked down into the sitting circle of the lifeboat lashed to the side of the ship and the light of day illuminated the orange rubber into an apparition of freedom.

Kel looked about and was glad to know that she was still alone despite her fantasy of escape. The men would be blackened by drunken sleep for a long time yet. It was perfect.

She had time. A minute to lower the boat and run back and grab the girl. She stepped into the shadows of the low-slung nothing-much sun and went quickly to unrope the boat and lower it into the water.

She went to work lowering the lifeboat from the crane, turning the crank with her thoughts set on the plan whilst her arms ached with the effort of heavy work. With each turn she cursed the salty seawater, the rust in every cable and on every cog.

With her mind racing crazy she didn't hear the laughter rumbling and rolling through the tin-can alleyways until it was too late.

'Looks like the stowaway's plannin jumpin ship!' shouted a low boom voice and Kel felt her insides crush with dread for the thing that was about to happen.

She turned to see the men for the first time clear as day. They laughed and grinned themselves into a circle.

'Leave me be,' she said calmly and she wished she had the girl ready and at arm's length of her dagger for the leverage she would have been.

'Let me through, lads,' called a voice from behind them. 'Let me through to see what it is you're seeing.'

The men unstuck shoulders and split for the captain. 'It's that crazy knife-wielder from last night, sir,' one of the younger men shouted.

Kel stood tall, ready for battle.

'Don't you know the law of the waves, girl?' he asked. 'Did nobody ever explain to you that stowaways get chucked off ship?'

Kel shrugged despite the bite of fear creeping up on her, and when the captain came close and closing she shrugged again and said 'no'.

'Hey lads, we've got a live one here haven't we?' He stood on his toes and huffed a hot acrid gut full of air into Kel's face. 'I suppose you've guessed by now that this ship isn't meant for runaway kids like yourself, your life is mapped out in the swamps.'

'I chanced upon it and fancied it just.' Kel looked him straight in the eye and pushed for pity the way little kids did.

'Is that right?'

'With all the latest happenins and goins on,' she continued, 'sposed the sea was the best place for goin.'

'You supposed right, but not on my ship.' The captain turned to the others and asked how it could be that there were two stowaways on board when each and every one of them had eyes in their head for looking and a gun in their hands for shooting.

Kel had a good look at the semi-auto rifles strapped

crossways to each man's shoulder and she had a fancy for one of those guns.

The man glared at her for the longest time and Kel glared back. There was no point in backing down, they either had her or they didn't.

'You're a kid,' he continued. 'Rough kid, but a kid all the same.'

Kel looked at the ground, found a bit of of dry gum to stub her toe against.

'So because of that fact, kid, I've decided to grant you armistice. Which to somebody like yourself means we're not going to throw you to the sharks, but you will remain locked up for the duration of the trip.'

'No,' said Kel. It wasn't supposed to be like this. America was useless to her without the drugs, without money. The drugs that awaited her and the swapsy girl coupled with the availability of the dinghy sitting pretty at the side of the boat were the only things she could think about.

The captain was talking again, going on and asking questions and whatever else, and Kel nodded and perhaps she spoke occasionally but inside she was tapping out time. She could feel the knife pushing hard against her hip-bone and it urged her to do something and to do something quick. She pushed her hat to the back of her head and felt for the six-inch blade through the material of her jacket.

'It beats me how nobody bothered to come up to my office and knock politely on my door to tell me that not only was my own flesh and blood stowed away onboard ship, but some rough-neck swamper too.' He turned toward Kel. 'So, I hear you've met my daughter?'

Kel's blood ran cold, they had found Rose after all. She watched Rose walk slowly through the crowd.

'My lovely daughter, good job my boys heard her shouting from the crate, said you had rescued her, by locking her up, imagine that.' He laughed and beckoned for her to move closer and Kel saw the girl's mouth twitch with amusement at the thought of Kel being found. When she saw the baby bundled in Rose's arms she looked at the ground, ashamed. She let her finger rest against the one-eye popper of her knife sheaf that hung from her belt and silently clicked it open, moved forward a little. What was she doing? It wasn't meant to be like this. Time slowly tapped out and before she knew it her hand was on the shank, she stepped forward toward the girl and put her free arm around Rose's neck, the knife pressed into the flesh. Kel stood still and the silence around them became deafening.

'Don't do anything stupid now,' said the captain. 'There's a baby settled there in Rose's arms, an innocent child.'

Kel shouted that she knew that already. She knew that he was trying to control her by threatening kin, the thing that was most important to most folk. But Kel was not most folk.

Kel held Rose tight and when she screamed and kicked out crazy Kel stiffened her grip and held her nerve and told the captain that she would be stealing the boat that dangled from the side of the boat and she pulled the girl backwards towards the dinghy and told her to quit her wailing mouth.

It was too late for more thinking or battling out a better plan otherwise and so she told them all to turn their backs and head to the other side of the ship to keep blood at bay and that her boss of sorts would be in touch.

In Kel's mind there was little doubt that she would use violence if needed. In the end survival came down to one thing and one thing only; kill or be killed.

Kel kept the knife settled to the girl's throat and she asked the men to give her a gun and ammo enough for her own protection and she told them that if they let her go nobody would come to any harm.

'You keep to your path to America and you won't have nothin to worry about.' She pulled the girl closer and told him that things would soon become clear.

'And what if we don't follow your stupid kid orders?' asked the captain.

Kel pushed the side of the knife a little more into the girl's throat.

'OK!' he shouted. 'Stop.' He told one of the men to place his gun on the deck in front of Kel.

'Good.' Kel reached out a foot and dragged the gun toward her and bent to it with the girl buckled beside her and picked it up. 'And just so you know,' she said, 'this int stupid kid orders, it's just orders.'

With the gun in hand and the knife still threatening the girl climbed down into the boat without fight and Kel stepped after her and she looked up toward the deck to see if the men had kept their promise of keeping to the other side. Some had but the captain had moved forward.

'What now?' asked Rose.

'Be quiet,' said Kel.

'But you're going to let me go, aren't you?' She was still smiling, enjoying the bit of excitement that Kel provided.

'No,' said Kel.

'But you said I'd be released.'

Kel looked at Rose for the longest time, she wanted to tell her that everything was going to be OK, but truth was the girl was far from it.

'I'm kidnappin you,' she said.

She settled the loaded gun in her lap and she told the girl not to move as she tightened her grip on the engine cord and pulled.

'You're what?' asked Rose again. Her smile was beginning to slip.

'Sorry.'

'*Sorry?* When are you planning my release?'

Kel shrugged and she said she supposed in a week or two, if Rose was lucky.

'What?' the girl shouted and Kel told her to shut it or else. Kel had her eye on the captain, he was calling for his men but they knew better than to get involved. When he hung from the side of the ship Kel told him to get back, stay back.

'What do you want with me?' shouted Rose. 'Why are you taking me from the ship?'

'I told you, I'm kidnappin you.' Kel stood to pull the cord

when she realised the boat was floating toward the back of the ship; she had to get the engine started and quick.

Kel bent to the cord and pulled and pulled but nothing started, and when she turned her gaze back to Rose she saw with panic rising that the girl had placed the baby into the floor of the boat and was lurching towards her. The motion pushed Kel's bit of the boat right toward the ladder at the end of the ship – easy for a man to scale down and come aboard. She could hear them up on deck, they were shouting and running the length of the vessel to see how far the lifeboat had drifted.

'You gonna get me shot,' Kel shouted. 'Get me shot and then what?'

'Good,' said Rose. 'I don't know why people like you always get away with things anyway.'

Kel grabbed the girl by her collar and started to shout, more words pouring from her in that one moment than most her whole life. 'The way you got your life int nothin to do with me,' she told her. 'Little rich-bitch girl with nothin but family and money on your side. It's people like *you* that's always gettin away with things. I've never got away with nothin, so just sit down will you?'

She gave the girl a push and the wave that reared up from the ship's belly had the girl tipped backwards into the water; a stupid girl with everything pink and stupid bobbing around her.

Kel pulled the motor cord one last time and to her relief the engine kicked and punched into life and she opened up the throttle. Behind them she could see the vessel moving slowly toward the horizon and she stared at it a long time until she was certain, the ship was on the move.

She returned her gaze to the boat and looked at the bundled baby that had started to cry at her feet and then at the girl in the water.

'Damn,' she said. 'Damn damn damn.'

'You stupid idiot,' yelled Rose when Kel raced the boat toward her. 'You stupid idiot girl, you could have got me killed.'

'Sit down,' shouted Kel as she yanked her fully into the boat.

She settled the shivering girl at the other end of the vessel, gave her a blanket and picked up the baby to soothe it shut for peace's sake.

In the distance Kel noticed that she could no longer see the ship, just the smudge of engine smoke where it had been. She breathed a sigh of relief and told herself this was worth it, it had to be.

Time passed. The girl sat mostly good and silent and brooding but on occasion she made a play for the gun, and those were the times when Kel showed her the blade of her knife and she was reluctant to have to flash it but what else was there. This was a job of sorts; she had work to be done and dusted and this is how they went through the short leaden night and on into the next day.

Chapter Four

Throughout the dull-dim morning the two girls sat opposed. Kel kept an eye on Rose from the back of the boat and when the girl returned her glare she looked toward the baby snuggled in blankets in the centre of the boat.

'You can't even look me in the eye can you,' said Rose.

Kel ignored her.

'Coward.'

Kel twisted a little more diesel into the engine. The noise put some distance between them as she wished the day away and for the dark to return for the sake of solitude.

'What kind of person steals another person?' Rose pushed forward in order to be heard.

'You should sleep some,' said Kel.

'I'm not tired.'

'If you sleep you'll feel better.'

'About what? You stole me.'

'Just for a bit.' Kel looked at the girl and told her that there was bread hidden in the bag at the bottom of the boat and that she could eat some of it if she liked.

'I think I'll pass, thanks.' Rose moved closer and Kel told her to sit back.

'Where are you taking me?'

'Mainland.'

'Why.'

'Cus it's part of the plan.'

'Not mine.'

Kel cleared her throat and she spat overboard. She wished she could have spat the girl out of the boat the same but she told herself to remember the plan. She reached for her bag and pulled out the compass and put it in her lap, found the coordinates on a piece of paper she kept in her jeans pocket. When the girl asked what she was doing she told her she was setting course for the mainland.

'Whereabouts on the mainland?'

'The docks.'

'Back to where we set off from?'

Kel ignored her, she didn't like the girl's attitude. Rose thought the plan was stupid but she didn't know the detail and why would she? The man at the river bar said Rose would be looked after until they received the guns from the captain, that she would be returned safely in good time. Kel could have told Rose this, but she realised the time it took the captain to return to Cornwall with the guns would be a long while yet, better to leave the girl to her ignorance. Whatever, that was all their business, all Kel needed to do was deliver the girl to the man from the river bar who would be waiting at the docks.

She kissed the compass and returned it to the bag. She was so close to completing her plan she could smell it, taste it on her lips, it was the flavour of success.

Kel looked at the girl and wondered if she was OK. She didn't like the silence, it unsettled her to know the girl had been all mouth onboard ship and now she was tight-lipped. She wondered if she gave Rose something of herself she might understand and she went to speak but her voice halted suddenly, words had a way of choking her. Nobody had ever given much mind to what she had to say in any case.

'I gotta get an operation,' she blurted finally.

'What?' The girl laughed and her sudden spite surprised Kel and she felt for the gun with her foot.

'Gotta get to America, get me some operation.'

'Why what's wrong with you?' The girl's eyes danced with delight and her candy-stick nails drummed on her mouth to keep from giggling again.

'My heart.' Kel couldn't believe she was giving something of herself away, she thought it might help but as soon as her words left her mouth she knew it was a big mistake and she kicked out in annoyance and told the girl not to laugh.

'I'm not, it just sounds a bit funny, the way you said it. How do you know you'll be able to get an operation in America?'

Kel shrugged and she told her you could buy whatever you wanted in South America, she had read about it.

'Like what?'

'A kidney, other organs I spose, whatever.'

'Even a new heart?'

'Maybe, or bits to make the one I got better.'

'I doubt it. Can't you get it fixed in the UK?'

'You're kiddin, int you? Swamp folk don't get operations, hospitals won't touch us, doubt if they would even if we did have money.'

'Well, I know you're poor because of the rags you're wearing but couldn't you just have just found someone rich to foot the bill?'

'You reckon?'

'I suppose not, but you could have gone around one of the towers, pleaded or whatever.'

'I int no beggar.' Kel wished she'd kept quiet.

'Oh God forbid that *that* was the case, but being a kidnapper is perfectly fine.' Rose started to giggle. 'It doesn't matter anyway, if you came around our tower I'd think you were a beggar, so.'

Kel looked the girl over; the pretty pink clothes at odds with her rough tongue.

Kel ignored her, she pushed out a foot to slide her bag toward the girl and she told her to eat something, put something in her mouth besides questions.

'Didn't you have anything to barter so you didn't have to steal someone?'

Kel looked at the baby and shrugged. 'Nothin,' she said.

'So what's in the bag besides bread?'

'Nothin much.'

'Nothing much of what?'

'Just bits and bobs stuff, nothin worth botherin bout.'

'Let me look.'

Kel watched the girl pull items from the bag like it was an unlucky dip. She began lining the things up on the seat beside her. 'Rain mac, lighter, lighter fuel, tobacco tins, water bottle, nappies, I'm guessing, pencils, more plastic bags and what's this? A notebook? Didn't think you could write, but whatever.'

Kel told her to stop and not to take anything else out of the bag and she grabbed the notebook and slid it down the side of her boot.

'What?' asked Rose. 'These are fine things to carry around, fine mementos from the swamps.'

Kel put out her hand, told the girl to take some bread if she wanted it but to return her things to the bag and the bag to her.

'I'll skip the bread, thank you.' Rose pushed the bag back toward Kel with her foot.

Kel opened the bag and tore a chunk of bread and split it two ways and passed one to Rose and told her to eat, that it was better to be full than hungry.

'We won't be long,' she said. 'Just gotta get in order to get gone.' The baby started to cry so Kel picked it up and passed it to Rose, told her to make herself useful and shut it up.

'*Get in order to get gone*, what does that even mean?'

'Get to where we're goin and then it won't be long till

you're home in your fancy tower.' Kel looked at the girl and she could see a little wild wind had picked up inside her, could see it whistling in her eyes.

'How long?' asked Rose.

Kel shrugged. 'Not long.' She wondered how long it would take the ship to get to America, buy the guns and about turn. It would be weeks at least.

'Like I said. Few days,' she lied. 'No more than a week.'

'And how do you know?' Rose asked.

'Cus that's the plan.'

'And how do you know I'll be OK?'

'I'll be round for a bit, I'll keep my eye on you.'

'No you won't, you'll be off to America to get your big paper-bag heart shrunk or whatever, and where will I be? Basement-bound no doubt, a hole in the ground or some place equally wonderful.'

'You'll be treated right.'

'Oh, yes, tied up and sedated probably so that freaks and cowpokes can come and do whatever they like with me.'

Kel backed up the motor for a little calm. She looked at the girl and she thought about the plan and how up to this point it didn't involve thinking of 'the goods' as a real person, she hadn't reckoned on that part of the deal. Rose was a living thing and despite her big mouth Kel supposed she didn't deserve more than a safe turnaround of events.

'I'll see to it that you're all right. I'll make em promise.' She nodded at the girl and with her honest eyes she told her that she meant it. Whatever it took, Kel would make sure that Rose was taken care of until she was safely exchanged for the contraband, the guns.

'Yes, well, I don't believe you.'

'Well you int got much choice in the matter.'

'OK.'

'OK. It won't be for long anyhow.' Kel looked out into the ocean and sighed, she was so close to getting what she wanted, so why did she feel so bad?

'Why didn't you catch me and head off earlier,' asked Rose, 'I mean, if we're having the conversation. Why did you wait two nights?'

'I couldn't find you.'

'Ha, that's funny, I should have hidden myself away for the duration. That would have messed things up big time.'

They sat in silence and Kel knew Rose was filtering and figuring things out and then suddenly she turned to Kel and asked if she had seen the sky.

Kel glanced up from the horizon. 'Gettin dark,' she said. 'Gettin dark with rain.'

'Getting dark with rain is an understatement. It takes a lot to sink a lifeboat, doesn't it?'

Kel nodded. 'Don't worry, we'll be there soon, int so far. Night and day is all. Put the mac on.' Kel didn't know what the fuss was all about, she hadn't bothered with the bind and gag, and anyway, the girl was already wet from falling into the sea.

'You don't know that,' said the girl. 'You don't know how far we've got to go. Didn't we just spend a couple of days at sea?'

'I know all what I got to do, got instructions for all of this.' Kel wished she could look at her notebook for reassurance but the girl was watching her, doubting her, making her look stupid. Rich people did that.

'A couple of days by ship versus forty-eight hours by speedboat, how does that even work?'

'We're smaller, lighter.'

'So?'

'Means we can go faster.'

Rose nodded, and Kel could tell she was pretending to think. 'Did you ever go to school?'

Kel ignored her.

'The ship's gotta be someplace soon enough, and your dad don't seem the type of man to be late on a delivery, especially what he got deliverin.'

'Furniture?'

'And the rest.'

'What?'

Kel sighed. 'Your dad runs guns if you dint know. He's not just the captain of a ship, he's a trafficker – a proper kingpin. That's just bout why you get to live the life you lead.'

Rose stared at Kel for the longest time and she asked her if she was serious.

'Why do you think I was asked to kidnap you?'

'Because my dad's rich? For ransom money?'

Kel shook her head. 'Money int worth the paper it's printed on for swamp folk. You got money and all and everyone thinks you stole it in any case. Guns is currency now, you can get a lot for guns.'

'I thought you were getting money to bring me wherever.'

'I'm gettin paid in goods.'

'What kind of goods?'

'Drugs.'

'What type?'

'I dunno. Drugs is drugs innit? I never ask.'

'Depends what you're into, how bad your life is.'

'I int into none but sellin. There int no other angle to this whole thing cept fixin up my heart so don't bother askin.'

'So you've decided to piss on other people's fireworks?'

Kel shrugged. Life wasn't fair however you looked at it, it sucked like a lemon every which way.

'You're just about as selfish as it gets. Hey, you're not one of those child pirates are you? I've heard about them.'

'Course not, just don't wanna die.' The truth suddenly made Kel flinch and her hand went to the knife for reassurance.

'She's not going to die,' said Rose to the baby that was waking in her arms. 'It seems to me like you've got along OK so far haven't you?'

Kel ignored her. Yes, no and whatever else was banging and bumping in her head.

'I mean, how do you know you have a heart problem anyway?'

'Born with it.'

'Yes, but how do you know?'

'Told it.' Kel leaned forward to pass the rain mac to Rose.

'By who?'

'Me folks.'

'How do they know?'

'Told it, and don't ask by who.' She caught Rose's eye and looked away.

'Does that mean you don't know either? Sounds like you've been fed a load of nonsense to me?'

Kel sighed. 'I was born with it and was a weak kid cus of it and all in it beats wrong and I know that cus I can feel it.' She looked up at the rain that was beginning to fall.

'You don't look like you were born a weak kid.'

'I was.'

Kel could tell the girl was thinking things through and she told her not to bother. 'I just was always meant to take things easy, not to go overexertin, even though my life int nothin but.'

'Ha. Well, I don't know why you're so bothered,' said Rose flatly. 'Life's just about as crap and boring as it is anyway: maybe you should accept defeat.'

'Got more fight in me than that.'

'Really? I think I'd just rather go out on one big party and then boom, go up in smoke. At least I'd die happy.' She leaned back so she could bounce the baby on her lap, it had started to cry.

'How you know?' asked Kel.

'What?'

'You'd die happy?'

'Girl, there's too much thinking about you, of course I'd die happy.' She looked at Kel and smiled, a little light returning to her eyes.

Kel looked away.

'So how old are you?'

'Fifteen.'

'Snap. So isn't it all about the partying, Keryn?'

'No, in the slums it's all bout survivin.' Kel looked at the whingeing baby and she wished she had the nerve to toss it overboard.

'I thought swamp kids had nothing to lose,' said Rose.

'We don't.'

'And everything to gain?'

'That int right.'

'Well that's sad,' said Rose. 'That's really stinking sad.'

Kel ignored her, the girl was smirking and Kel was filled with the passion for pushing. She wished the girl gone, gone into the water and down as deep as the ocean floor.

'Aw, now I've gone and upset the kidnapper,' said Rose and Kel knew the girl's eyes were skirting toward the gun that she had lodged behind her legs.

'Won't do you no good to think bout it,' Kel said.

'What? What am I thinking about?'

'The gun, escapin, whatever.'

'It hasn't even crossed my mind; there's nothing better than being up close and personal with a stinking swamp kid.'

Kel told her to shut up and she turned her ear away from Rose's sarcastic run of mouth. It wasn't humour and if it was it was the worst kind. The girl was all spikes and spears and barb, Kel couldn't wait to offload her and she put her mind to the motor and let the sea spray splash across the bow as they pushed forward.

Night came in a slow-slip stretch and Kel was glad when it was finally pulled and tucked neatly about them. She could stare headlong into its yawning gape and take comfort in infinity. Forget about the girl a moment, forget about the baby.

In the dark night Rose was nothing to her, the girl's prying eyes just blown-out stars and her dancing tongue silenced in sleep.

Time eclipsed the two girls racing in the boat. Night followed day followed night. They didn't speak except to ask for the passing of food or water. Bar feeding and changing time Kel ignored the baby when it cried and on those ear-piercing occasions Rose would sigh and click her tongue and gather it up into her arms for petting.

Kel told herself that it wouldn't be long now. She tag-tailed the stars the way she had been told so she knew well the way in which they were heading. She could see the barricade of coastline in the distance, the curve of headland as they finally entered the bay.

Through the blue of dark light Kel could see the silhouettes of the dock buildings, the cranes and winches swinging into view and behind that the towers stood like shadows haunting the higher ground. She imagined the swamps and her own swamp forest lying off behind and it made her sick thinking about it, her mind returned there and she wished it hadn't.

'I can see the towers,' said Rose suddenly.

'Can't miss em.'

'But something doesn't look right.'

'You only just realised? Things int bin right for forever.'

'The lights, stupid.'

'What lights?'

'The towers, where are all the lights?'

Kel slowed the boat and looked and as she looked she felt the buzz of a job well done seep away. The horns were the first thing that reached their ears. They burst from the water like tiny explosions springing from the sea bed and were angled at every turn.

'What's going on?' asked Rose.

'I don't know.' Kel let the engine bubble some and stood when she saw lights firing up and growing on the mainland and she knew that these were not the glitter-ball glow of harbour lights. The world that she had only recently left behind had been washed clean by firelight and the constant wet earth dried bright, beautiful.

Kel swallowed hard, fearful.

The first part of the plan was so close to completion. Why this? Why now?

She watched Rose settle the baby into a circle of blanket in the bed of the boat and then took down the oil lamp from its staff above their heads. The girl held it up toward Kel's face as if to check the expression there and then she put it to her lap and cradled it like it was the only thing worth knowing in the world.

'I don't think I like this,' Rose said suddenly. 'I don't think I like this at all.'

Kel didn't speak. She couldn't: all she could think about was her plan, all she could see was it slip from her hands and slowly fall away.

'What do you think is going on?' asked Rose.

'I said I don't know.'

'You've changed.'

'How's that?'

'I can smell fear on you.'

'That int fear,' said Kel as she sat back down.

'You think something's heading our way?'

'I know it,' said Kel and with one hand she slowed the boat to a nothing speed and with the other she felt for the gun. She watched the dock for the usual line of boats but it was all motion – what vessels weren't tearing away full pelt from the docks were bobbing and listing rudderless in the bay. She remembered how things were on the land days earlier. She had thought it was another low-level riot but now she wasn't so sure.

'I can hear screaming,' shouted Rose.

Kel turned her head out of the wind, she could hear it too.

'And look,' Rose leaned forward of the boat with the lamp dangling close to the water, 'there's people everywhere.' She looked back at Kel in horror. 'You see them?'

Kel nodded. Yes she saw them, a dozen plus screaming heads and flailing arms floating in the distance, grappling at the sucking, vacuum sea.

'They're getting closer,' said Rose.

'No they're not.

'They are, they're floating towards us.'

Kel sat forward and focused, suddenly she could see them all; some bodies moved on their own accord, others bobbed like bottle corks, directionless.

'I see em.' She looked at Rose and nodded in disbelief.

The land that Kel hated and loved in equal measure was burning out of control and the people she may or may not have known were in and on and everything about the ocean. The bodies stretched all the way back to the docks and jammed between the boats, Kel knew it would be impossible to navigate.

'There's no way through,' she said. They sat in silence and the dark kept them and slung fog and rain into the mix; enough of hell on earth to make Kel feel like screaming too.

'We've got to help them,' said Rose.

'We can't.'

'They're going to die.'

'There's too many people.' Kel tipped the boat a little ready for the turn, they had drifted too far into the bay and had reached the first of them. A boy no older than them was trying to hook himself to the back of the boat and his pulling and punching had the tiny vessel threatening to go under.

'Get off,' shouted Kel, 'you're gonna pull us in.' She let the engine shudder to a stop and reached across to unpeel his pinching fingers and as she did so she saw the compass that had been beside her on the seat bounce out of the boat and into the sea.

'Help!' shouted Rose. 'We're trapped.'

Kel looked across to the front of the boat to see more fingers grip the side of the boat, it was in danger of capsizing.

'We're going to go under.' Rose looked at her in horror.

'No we int,' Kel reached into the floor of the boat to grab the gun and she raised it and fired it into the ocean. One and then two and then a dozen more for luck. Each time the bullets hit the water it rocked them close to the hell that was fingering them under and the fierce heads and hands that crawled toward them.

'We gotta get gone,' said Kel.

She yanked the cord over until the motor kicked into life and she spun the boat away and flying from the carnage until the only scream was coming from the baby in the centre of the boat.

Out into the dead of night and back into the unknown; two girls and the tiny baby with nothing but questions circled around them.

Now what?

Kel hoped the girl wouldn't start up with the why why why so she could take a moment to think straight. She couldn't stand to hear Rose's questions and more than that she didn't have any answers.

How could she, when she didn't know what had happened on the mainland? It could have been anything or it could have been nothing. All Kel knew was her plan as she'd plotted it was dead in that same water, she needed time to set it on a new course. She felt in her boot and took out her notebook and pushed it into her back pocket.

'So what now, swamper? Surely that wasn't part of the plan?'

'All I know is we gotta get away. We'll head down the coast a little, find a quiet bay to pull the boat in.'

'And then what?'

'Walk the coast path back to the docks.'

'Hell, why? Didn't you just see what I saw?'

'Yes, but I gotta get back there.'

Rose sat back and folded her arms. 'I get it. You're still planning on handing me over. After everything we've just seen. Brilliant.'

Kel turned to the stern of the boat, let a little more fuel into the engine.

'Brilliant,' continued Rose. 'Just brilliant.'

Kel ignored her, there were still options available to her, of course there were, she was so close to finishing the deal. She had kidnapped the girl, the hardest part was over.

'Things will soon be back to normal.' Kel looked at the girl and nodded.

'Do you think so?' asked Rose. 'I mean really?'

'I know so, probably just an explosion on the docks, happens all the time.'

'And the people in the water?'

'Panic is all, it'll be over soon enough.'

'If that's so, why are we heading down the coast?'

'To be on the safe side.' Kel looked at Rose and nodded. 'Everythin will be fine.' It was to herself that she said this. Small-scale unrest or a catastrophic uprising she didn't know.

'But all of those people,' said Rose.

'Don't think about it.'

'What happened, really?'

'I told you already.'

Something was wrong with the engine and Kel bent to listen.

'Things can't get too much worse right now, can they?' said the girl and she bent to pick up the baby and cuddled it close.

'I dunno.' Kel slowed the motor, its ticking was off.

'What is it? What's wrong?'

'The engine int right.' It was spluttering and jumping sporadic.

'What you mean the engine isn't right?'

'It's as I say.'

'But it was fine.' Rose crawled forward toward her.

'Maybe somethin happened back there, somethin got stuck or somethin.'

'What like? Oh God, maybe an arm or a leg.'

'Maybe a bit of clothin, all sorts was floatin round, why you gotta think the worst?'

'Oh I don't know, maybe because the worst just happened? Can you tell me otherwise?'

'Bout what?'

'Is the engine bust?'

Kel pulled out the throttle a little but it was no good and the cord sat long and loose in her hand. No matter how she tried to start it over, the motor was no more.

'Is it?' asked Rose.

'Yes,' said Kel. 'The engine's bust.'

Chapter Five

Kel was always running from something. Running from or running toward, but in any case it was all escape. Escape from the here and now, from the world she inhabited within and the world that bullied her from the outside.

The two girls sat in the deep dark down at opposite ends of the boat. Kel dug and stretched the oars into the ocean like her life depended upon it because it did. She bent toward the water, sweating and paining in the battle. She looked at the girl and the girl looked away.

'Just so you know, it's your fault,' said Rose. 'Everything – and I mean everything – is your fault.'

Kel ignored her and she rested the oars on her legs and sat up to inspect the coastline in the dark but it was all rock.

'You've decided not to talk now, have you? Mouth like a gun and then nothing.'

'Int got nothin,' said Kel. She shrugged off the ache in her arms and continued with the one-two one-two rowing, keeping one eye on the burning horizon they floated away from.

'Wish there was one place close we could go in,' Kel admitted at last. There might still be time to get to land, return to Falmouth via the cliff path, get back on track. But the tide was against them. However far Kel thought they had gone the waves dragged them back and what progress they made was taken from them.

'Could just be the calmest place on earth,' said Rose suddenly and she sat back to watch the sea pull them further out to sea. 'Calm if we hadn't seen what we just saw.'

Kel wished the girl would be quiet awhile, it was getting harder to keep the dinghy close to land. She leaned from the side of the slippery boat to slap water on to her face, made a point of ignoring her companion because there were things she needed to set straight in her own mind.

'We're not getting anywhere,' Rose said, shaking her head and Kel noticed the slow-crawl panic as it slunk from the pool of lamplight and into her eyes. 'We're stranded.'

Kel continued to dangle from the little orange boat. In the lamplight the water was all the shades of black-blue-green and as calm as level card.

She ran the water in finger cups to the blisters that were forming on her palms and then leaned back and kept a hand trailing for the beauty of the sea just being, closed her eyes for a moment's rest. The effort of the past few days had her beat. Her arms hurt from rowing, her eyes ached from staring down the dark.

'You're not going to sleep are you?' asked Rose.

'I won't.' Kel snatched her hand from out of the water and sat up. She looked up at the sky and wished there was moonlight for guiding but there was none. The black of forever night was up and down and everywhere complete. She took up the oars again.

'So what now?' asked Rose. 'Like what really and not just bull.'

'We'll head down the coast a bit, as I said before,' said Kel. 'Down the coast and see what's what. That hasn't changed.'

'But how long will it take us to get to someplace that isn't water?'

Kel shrugged and said she didn't know and she wished the girl would quit with the words awhile.

'And nothing but oars for rowing.' said Rose. 'I guess your plans are truly scuppered now we've got no engine, I could give thanks for that if nothing else.'

Kel kept her mind on the rowing and when Rose finally grew quiet Kel took that to mean she was settling somewhere toward peace.

'Sorry,' said Kel finally. The word did not belong to her and it dangled from her tongue in a pincer-grip. 'I'm sorry,' she said again.

Kel kept from looking at the girl because she knew she was crying but there was nothing more she could do or say except that Rose should try for some sleep and she would continue to row through the night and she set right about it.

Her eyes stayed on the horizon until it tempted her with the promise of colour; a new day dawning, drawing itself into their picture.

She'd been rowing she didn't know how long when she felt her heart shudder and stop a moment and she held her breath and waited for it to fall back to beating. If she could've reached down into the cavity to squeeze it back to size she would have done so. Have it grow good and strong in her hand, tell it she had a future planned for it, a map drawn that featured happiness if it would just hold on a minute.

The place Kel had set secret for herself was a bit of dry fantasy scrubland far from the road, and a truck to ride out on that land that would be hers and nobody else's. In her imagination she had her own piece of land for food and wood for heat and shelter and with nobody around to know her, because those who did would try to take it away.

She supposed this was her dream, the dream she carried with her since childhood.

But now all hope and fear and everything else between lay out there, beneath the fractal this-way that-way any-way surface of the water. Her destiny distilled into small drops of chance. She was at the tide's mercy and that of the changing winds and the craggy, cagey moon.

Whatever would be would be and if anything like a revelation had ever happened in Kel's mind it happened in that instant; perhaps to live in the moment was the only way to live at all. All else was wasting time wallowing in self-pity when things didn't go the way of imagination. To plan was to fail at the first stage. Better to be bobbing mindless in a boat than be running and planning and getting it all wrong.

All bets were off. She was stuck with a girl who she didn't like and unable to get to shore and everything that was wrong about her life was still in it and worse.

Kel brought the oars into the boat a moment and slid her hand up her sleeve to feel the comfort scars but found no solace there and she wished for the privacy that would enable her to cut through skin just a little, to let out heat and steam off the pressure that was building within.

She crossed her hands quick into her lap and focused on the waves and to the song the girl had started singing to the baby beneath her breath. Kel listened to it from start to finish and the beauty concealed within it made her wish for everything she had never known.

'You make that song up?' she asked.

'I suppose so.'

'You got a nice voice,' said Kel. 'More un nice.'

The girl shrugged and said it was just a voice.

'Still,' said Kel.

Rose sat up and nodded toward the horizon. 'I'm glad to see daylight coming.'

Kel agreed.

'Have you been rowing all night?'

'Best part.'

'Where are we?'

'Further down the coast.'

'You think we'll be able to get in?'

Kel shook her head.

'You must be tired.'

'I'm OK.' Kel sat forward and took up the oars and put them back into the water. To be rowing was to be doing something better than nothing.

A little of the early rising rainbow sky danced on the surface of the sea and when Kel split the oily surface with the oar the colours divided into the depths like fish from another, friendlier dimension.

'You look tired,' said Rose again. 'You can take a break if you want, sleep or whatever, I'll take over.'

'I'm fine.' Kel pointed toward where the rising sun was meant and told her companion that at least they knew which way was east.

'Is that good?'

'If we know east then we know west the same, Cornwall isn't so far away, if we keep pushin against the tide we'll hit land eventually.'

'Shame you lost the compass.'

'We lost the compass.'

'Is that right. So which way are we heading?'

Kel thought for a moment. 'South-west,' she said. 'We're headin south-west.' She bent to the sea to splash herself alert with the water and kept at it until her hands became cuts of deadbeat meat. She could hear Rose talking about food and hunger and dying and she kept her face to the water a moment longer.

'We've got to eat something,' said Rose when Kel sat up, 'What else do you have in your bag besides bread?'

'Nothin.'

'Well that's good. Great, in fact. I thought you were a planner? Not much planning involved here.'

'We weren't meant for long at sea.'

'So we starve. Brilliant.'

Kel looked out at the ceaseless sea. 'No,' she said. 'We fish.'

'With what?'

'Hook and line.'

'You got a hook and line?'

Kel nodded and she pulled her bag toward her and tipped the contents until she found the tin she was looking for.

'At least one of your swamp momentos might prove useful.'

Kel ignored her and set about rolling a pinch of bread between her finger and thumb and threading it to the hook and she passed a corner of the loaf to the girl and Rose thanked her and they sipped a little from the only canteen of water between them.

When Kel had finished chewing on the blunt stale bread she asked Rose if she had a maid back home to cook her food like most tower folk.

'Maybe I did,' said Rose.

'What was she called?'

'Mother.' Rose smiled and the way she laughed made Kel not like her all over again. 'She does most things. So, are you going to throw that line out?'

Kel checked the bait and then lowered it into the gobbling gloom and sat back.

'Do you think we'll catch anything?' asked Rose.

'Maybe we'll get lucky.'

'If I was a praying girl I'd pray, but I'm not so I won't.'

'Neither am I.'

'What?'

Kel looked up at the bedraggled girl, the pink of her dress drab with dirt and water. 'A prayin girl.'

'Well at least we've got one thing in common. Just one, mind.'

Kel shrugged, she could see in the girl's run-rabbit eyes that she had questions jumping all over, ready to be asked.

'So fresh out of the bogs are you?'

'You know that already,' said Kel.

'And *your* mum? I'm sure she's no stranger to the swamp.'

Kel shrugged. 'My life int for tellin.'

'That's stupid, everyone's got a backstory, family and all that jazz.' Rose did the stupid laugh thing that she seemed to like and then asked for more detail.

'Well I got folks, that's all you need to know.'

'Oh the same folks who told you you're going to die because of your heart, which is probably just bullshit? What are they like other than liars?'

'I int tellin more un that.'

Kel thought about her life spent in the shack in the swamp woods and how funny it would be to tell the dumb-spoilt daddy's girl the truth. Funny and strange and painful in a way that made her heart stop almost complete because she had never once told her story out loud. To put the words up and out on to the wind would be like waving a blood-stained flag all around. Holding up her sins and the sins of others to an unsuspecting world.

She looked at Rose and told her not to worry in any case, but the girl was in the mood to press Kel further in regards to her life. Kel was or wasn't guilty of the things Rose thought, but she knew guilt was what was written on her face: over fifteen years of living it had become her expression, and no matter how hard she worked it calm, a recognisable evil crawled out of the mirror. She had her father's eyes. Beautiful eyes, dark and haunted with the memory of what she had seen and what she might see in coming years.

She sat up and stretched to look deep down into the ocean and wondered what she must have looked like to the eyes and minds of the things that lived there. Another world entirely watching as the orange boat pitched and rolled above it. Then she turned her attention to the blisters on the palms of her hands, the skin had rubbed and slid and re-stuck wrong and the wounds wept for stop.

'How are they?' asked Rose.

'Skinned,' said Kel and she took off her shirt and pulled the knife from her belt to slice the cuffs into strips and she wrapped two around her hands and gave Rose the others and it was like this that they took turns to row west, to row out the cold, damp day down into a night puddle.

Out there somewhere and not too far from reach was the Cornish coast, Kel told herself not to forget this. She told herself if her plan was gone she would have to construct another. If they could just get to land and make it back to her swamp district, back to the river bar and the man. Wouldn't he know what was going on? He would be expecting her to turn up better late than never, didn't he say she was good for her word?

She pulled her notebook from her pocket, waited for inspiration to come. When it didn't she sighed and put it back.

A few hours drifting and sleeping in the rockaby boat and then onwards towards the fading light as they traced the absent sun's hidden rays like deadbeat dogs sniffing out a kill. To go at something was to have it eventually, no matter the exhaustion that had them salted with burning blisters and their tongues wiggle from their lips like desert worms. They were heading somewhere whether they liked it or not; wherever the tidal shift and the passing change in wind fronts decided for them.

More passing hours and no sight of land, and Kel realised that if they stopped to think and search for a conclusion to their ocean existence they would find nothing close to resembling reason. They were alone. Alone and adrift at sea with nothing but the occasional splash of waves against the side of the boat. Alone and tired and for the girl perhaps a little confused. Rose's high life had been one thing and that great height thing had fallen and fallen hard. One minute you're someone with money and a house full of stuff and the next you're nobody with nothing and a boat full of empty.

Kel's life on the other hand had always been empty and now was just as empty but for the needy baby and the useless girl and the useless bouncing boat. Empty as before when she might have died from beatings or the stupid faulty heart. Only difference was now she was a hundred times more likely to die. Die and be dead in the supping sea with the girl on her dead-soul conscience forever.

A day and a night and a day again they went at the one thing and the only thing that would save them and keep them sane. Hope. Kel said it over in her head and she put it into the wind like a rescue flag flapping for all to see and all to hear. Hope for living and for the safety of. It was the thing that had them in the morning when light came peeping and at night when the stars appeared again to point Kel right. Land was out there somewhere, if she just knew in which direction to point them.

In the early mornings Kel gathered the inch of rainwater collected in the creases of the boat and tipped it into her tin canteen and checked the line she set for chancer fish but there were none. Soon they would eat the last of what was edible from the bottom of her saddle bag; a bit of something but mostly a bit of nothing much at all.

At night she took the steering shift for her knowing of stars and some time she spent rowing but mostly she lay with an oar dipped in the water to act as rudder and let all of which she could not control carry them forward, the boat a nothing floating thing with kids aboard rocking out a makeshift idea of rescue and hope.

Kel supposed she should feel something about what it was to still be alive, to be breathing was one good. Sitting and breathing and looking to the come again go again stars was all in all right.

On one late night or was it early morning Kel looked at the stars a long time. They told her where to go and there was comfort in that too, to know what it was to be the right way up when sky and ocean mirrored each other so perfectly. The thin cotton line of the horizon that stitched the two together was black on black, but it had shadow enough in its ether that Kel could still place it. To have that perspective was to know that land still existed somewhere. They would get to the destination fate had planned eventually. They had to, they had come this far.

'What are you looking at?' asked Rose suddenly.

'The horizon just.'

'You see anything other than black?'

Kel shook her head. 'Nope,' she said.

'You catch anything worth eating?'

'Nope again.'

Rose sighed and she put the baby she had been petting into its makeshift cradle that was nothing more than a burlap twist of sack and she sat up and lit the lamp and then set about rinsing through the nappy rags as something to busy herself with.

'Don't tell me we need to save the oil,' she said.

'I won't.'

They sat in silence, nothing to do and nothing to be done except sit and wait for the night to end, but at that moment Kel wondered if daylight would ever return.

Chapter Six

'Hey,' shouted Rose suddenly, 'I see something.'

Kel jumped to her feet, making the boat rock. 'What?' She steadied herself to look to where the girl was pointing.

'Over there, just keep looking and you'll see it.' Rose blew out the lamp. 'It's a light flashing on and off.'

Kel stared into the night and she kept her eyes from blinking until she spotted it.

'What do you think?' asked Rose. 'It's something isn't it?'

Kel nodded and then she said yes, it was something.

'What?'

'A trawler I reckon.' It was hard to make it out through the rain.

'Doesn't look much like a trawler to me.'

Kel about turned the boat so she could have a better look 'It's on its side, that's what you can see, its light's in-out the water.'

'Are you sure?'

Kel was sure and she started to row toward the arch of hull and all the time she wished its crew dead long and short enough that they could find food, and after food all the things that might make their life at sea more bearable.

She took her time to row the boat close to the trawler and she told Rose to be quiet and swaddle the baby the same until they knew for sure that they were alone. Something had happened to the vessel and it had happened recently, the mast light shining bright meant the battery was still charged and running.

'What do you reckon?' whispered Rose.

'I reckon I don't know more un you.'

'About the boat I mean, what happened.'

'Ran into somethin. Relight that lamp and put it forward so we don't do the same.'

'Like what? It isn't like there's any rocks about.'

'Just do it.'

Rose lay forward of the dinghy with the lamp outstretched to the water and both girls held their breath.

'I wouldn't like to think what's down there,' said Rose suddenly. 'Wouldn't like to think what's at the bottom of the ocean at all.'

Neither did Kel but she kept her thoughts to herself.

'Do we have sharks around here?'

'Don't worry they int the type to tip boats.'

'But we do have sharks.'

Kel ignored her and told her to keep looking for signs of life and she dug the oars into the water in order to circle the trawler. She called out to anyone that might have been half-sunk along with it that they were here to help if help was what was needed, but nothing but the sound of water in all its guises called back.

'I swear if I see another dead body I'm going to swing,' said Rose.

'Swing for who?'

'You, I'm going to swing for you.'

They circled the boat three times and there was nothing for it then but to pull in and climb aboard. Go seek and find something more than the nothing they had in hand.

'I'll climb up,' said Kel as she brought the boat up into bumping distance. 'I'll climb and you steady and secure the boat.' She threw Rose the rope.

'And then what? Am I just supposed to sit and wait?'

Kel nodded and said that was near enough it.

'What if I paddled off, what then?'

'You wouldn't.'

'You know me well enough to know that, do you?'

Kel stood and looked at the girl and the girl stood the same. They were becoming more connected than two girls at war. Somehow and without warning the gap between them had shortened and they were growing close to equal in the battle. It was something Kel had not reckoned on. 'Well?' asked the girl, her blue eyes flotsam floating somewhere in the ocean.

'Well what?'

'Are you going to let me on board or are you going to risk my running off?'

Kel knew the girl didn't have it in her to run, but maybe she had as much right as any to do what she pleased. Until things got back on track, that was, or Kel could see enough of the track to pursue it.

'Come on then,' she said finally, 'but don't forget, I'm still in charge.'

They secured the boat with the one coil rope that came with the dinghy and Kel was the first to climb. She took her time to navigate the near vertical deck for anything worthy of a finger or toe for climbing and then told Rose to watch what she was doing if she was coming and to bring the lamp and tie the baby to her back. Kel opened the door with the glass still in it and lowered it sideways to the deck and she crouched before entering and flicked on her lighter so she could take in her surroundings.

The control panel and everything that was useful was useful no more and it formed a wall in front of her. What had been navigationally useful was either stop-clocked or on the ground. Kel put her boot to the floor that once was a clapper-board wall. Everything was broken at just about every angle.

'Nothin,' she said to herself and she bent to the cupboards and every door was padlocked shut. She stood and kicked about some more and looked down at their orange bubble boat and saw that Rose was gone.

Kel sighed and climbed back out from the upturned box of nothing and hung on to its frame to look for the girl.

'Rose?' she shouted. 'You better not be dead in the water cus that int the plan.'

'You would know if I was,' shouted the girl and Kel couldn't help but smile. Rose was so annoying it sometimes reflected back as a form of entertainment and she wasn't used to that.

'Where are you?' Kel shouted.

'Below board.'

Kel looked for the hatch and it was in the middle of the boat and she took her time to swing from the starboard railings one and then two toward the opening.

'Are you coming?' shouted Rose. 'I've got food if you're interested, real food.'

Kel climbed through the hole and slid past the wooden steps.

'So what do you reckon?' asked Rose and she sat on what used to be the side of the counter with the lamp settled in amongst packets of dried food.

'Looks like you found somethin worth findin.'

'It does, doesn't it? If we could find something to cook them on and in that would be even better.'

Kel stepped closer so she could see what the pokey room had to offer and there was something there in the detail that had her think they weren't the only ones to have bothered the place recently.

'Did you find anything for us upstairs?' asked Rose.

Kel shook her head and something odd went through her that she wasn't sure was good or bad, she'd never been part of an us except as a gang and that was the Crows and that wasn't good. She watched Rose pile up the food and she put it all into categories and it mostly went savoury, sweet, other.

'We should pack that lot up,' said Kel, 'pack it up and whatever else and head out.'

'Out where?' asked Rose. 'I'm staying put.'

'Out and on, keep tryin to get back to the mainland.'

'I don't know about you but right now my place is right here. The bigger the boat the better the rescue.'

'I got a bad feelin bout this, better to get out and get gone.'

Well it might be bad for you, but it's the better option for me wouldn't you say?' Rose jumped from the counter and set about upturning stools for sitting and making good.

'We int stoppin here tonight,' said Kel and then she said it again to put a bit of authority back into the situation.

'If you want to know I'm looking for a gas stove or something similar,' Rose continued. 'You can look too if you want, if you're not too busy, and a pan would be great, we need a pan.'

Kel looked around at the nothing much of anything that cluttered the room. 'Can't we just eat whatever that int rot and go?'

Rose sat down on one of the stools and everything about her looked normal everyday in a world that was three-quarters turned. 'Don't you want cooked food?' she asked. 'Perhaps you really were born of savages, perhaps that's it.'

91

Kel sat down and she kept her mouth shut because the girl knew the answer well enough.

'We could make a fire,' continued Rose. 'If we had a fire we would be halfway to eating something good.'

Kel looked around and saw a cupboard with its door tented at the side and she went and pulled the pots that lived there to the floor.

'What size you want?' she asked Rose.

'Depends what size fire you're willing to make.'

'Not too big.'

'Maybe we shouldn't. Maybe it's too dangerous seeing the boat has run aground or whatever, isn't it likely it leaked diesel everywhere?'

'Good point, but we should collect up as much fuel as we can find anyway,' said Kel. 'For the lamp or whatever.'

'And what about the fire?'

'What bout it?'

'Dangerous?'

Kel thought for a moment. 'Wait, I saw somethin outside.'

She passed Rose the biggest pan and dragged a stool to stand on so she could climb back out of the hatch.

'Where are you going now?' shouted Rose.

'I seen somethin worth havin.' She kicked off the side-swipe stairs and pulled herself back up on to the slippery deck.

The night sky remained full of stars and they studded the black with a billion blunt bullets. Kel clipped her heels to the edge of the hatch and lay back on to the deck to contemplate a minute for one minute's sake and she noted the stars in relation to the boat so if morning came upon them suddenly she would be able to work some kind of journey into the thing from there. Out there in the core of the nowhere ocean it was as if the world and all its worries and wars had fallen away and what was left was the yawning cavity where nothing existed accept silver-bell stars. Space for thinking and counting out time that no longer bore relevance. Life had clocked off, stopped.

Kel sighed and her breath let off something akin to a loaded gun. The things that didn't matter to her in normal circumstance mattered to her now and she knew this was because of the girl. The girl who was a nobody had in a scattering of days become somebody, proof that the solitary life Kel'd had settled in her mind's eye for so long was the right one and she knew she couldn't look after the girl much longer. That she needed to get rid as soon as possible.

What if her plan was not going to work? She would have to find someone with enough kindness in them to take the girl until things softened down, get her back home to her mum in Cornwall and her tower life. Maybe the girl would keep the baby, she seemed to like it well enough.

Kel could start over then, head to America in any case and find a job running drugs, save enough for the operation or die trying, it was a coin flip but at least her destiny was hers alone.

She pushed off from the deck when she heard Rose calling and clambered and crawled the best she could until she reached the steel pail she'd noticed earlier and she tossed it into the hole. Then she went about pulling and prying the planks of wood aboard the boat that were loose and coming up and these she threw below deck too.

'You could have had me knocked to the ground with a nail shot through my skull,' shouted Rose. 'Or my foot. Haven't you noticed I don't have shoes?'

'Int no nails in the wood,' said Kel as she jumped back into the cabin, 'and it int my fault you took to wearin heels onboard ship.'

'What do you call this then?'

Kel looked up to see a six-inch spike poking her way.

'Keep that,' she said. 'Keep any nails you find, em could be useful.'

'For what exactly?'

'Anythin.'

They set about stomping the planks into halves and quarters and Kel hammer-split the wood with her knife until they had enough for a fire and there was water good for drinking straight and water good for boiling from a tap on the wall. Kel checked its reserves and there were ten litres left in the tank at the very least.

'We should take that with us,' she said to Rose.

'What?'

'The water tank.'

Rose agreed and when they had a small fire sparking in the bucket and water boiling for pasta they looked closer at their environment.

'Pots are good, let's take them too,' said Rose as she searched through the detritus with the lamp in hand. 'Any kind of container would be handy.'

Kel stood back and watched the girl come alive with purpose. She wasn't afraid to work after all. 'And anythin that can be set alight,' Kel added, 'things like rags are handy for flares.'

'And all the food,' continued Rose. 'It would be good not to starve to death. How long would it take?'

'To what?'

'Starve to death?'

'Bout three weeks I reckon.'

'That long?'

Kel shrugged and said maybe less.

Rose sat opposite from Kel and the fire whilst the bundled baby slept sound against her back and she asked if they would ever get back to Cornwall.

'Course,' said Kel, 'I told you, we int far, don't reckon anyway, just need a good current.' With the tide in the right direction it would be a short stretch around the tip of the coast and north where maybe things weren't so bad. Maybe even the docks didn't have so much disaster to them now: the possibility of things returning to normal was realistic enough for Kel to think it and believe. The thing that had happened might have been just that, a thing or a situation run wrong that had started out as panic but had then come back around. It was always like that, one side struggled whilst the other landed on their feet. No matter the situation, Kel knew those people floundering in the water would have been swamp folk.

Suddenly Rose made her jump by asking her what was wrong besides the obvious.

'Nothin.' Kel shrugged and she watched the pasta water froth and fall from its hooked perch above the flames.

'Doesn't look like nothing.' Rose poked the pot with a fork and they both sat back to watch more droplets spittle and die out on the heat.

'Are you thinking about back there? All those people drowning.' She looked Kel straight in the eye and said it was OK to feel sad or maudlin or whatever.

'I int maudlin,' said Kel and that was the truth, she couldn't care any which way about the people.

'Well I'm just saying, it's OK to feel something if you're already feeling it.'

'I int feelin nothin.' She looked at Rose and sighed. 'Feelin int my thing.'

'Or thinking it, you're allowed to think things too.'

Kel leaned forward and plucked herself a twist of pasta and she ate it and said the pot was nearly ready.

'You don't have to act so tough just because, it doesn't hurt to show your worries. It's not a sign of weakness.'

'Course it is.'

'Of course it's not, it's just emotion, one way of making sense of things.'

Kel cleared her throat. 'Spose I int got no emotion to me then, that's fine, I can live with that.'

'Well you shouldn't.'

'Why not?'

'Because it's not normal.'

'Well then that's me and all, not normal and no emotions and whatever else, you got enough drippin for all of us in any case. Can we eat now?'

'Whatever you want, dear kidnapper.'

'Cus we int eaten in forever.'

Rose sat forward to take the pot for draining and she said she knew Kel was changing the subject and that was fine with her. They sat in silence whilst they ate the bite and chew pasta from tin bowls and it had never tasted so good.

When the pasta was gone and their stomachs stretched to capacity Kel stabbed open a tin of peaches with her knife and they sucked at their flesh and kissed them like they were summer-day drift-away ice-pops. To have fruit and any fruit was to have new-found life returned to their bones and blood and colour put back into their thinking.

Yep, Kel thought, maybe things would not be so bad, she'd start over once the girl was gone. Throw herself at any crime that would pay towards the operation, as long as it didn't involve kidnap.

She would draw the line at dealing in people, it was messy. And besides, people talked back.

'What are you smiling about?' asked Rose. 'And don't say it's the peaches because I won't believe you.'

Kel swung her stool up against the side of the boat that used to be the ceiling so she could recline.

'Just thinkin I've good as had it with kidnappin after this.'
She lit herself a cigarette and smoked some and then she
passed it to Rose.

'Really? You sure?'

Kel shrugged.

'Does this mean I'm free to go?'

'No, I said after this. Don't know how you'd get gone even
if I let you.'

Rose pretended to be thinking things over. 'I'd take the
boat.'

'The dinghy?'

'It is mine.'

'It's your dad's.'

'Ha, mine, my dad's, it's all the same. It certainly isn't
yours. But you can have this crash and burn wreck if you
want.'

Kel said that was fine by her. And all the things that came
with it.

'You wouldn't get the food.'

'Hell I would, if this is my boat then all and everythin
aboard is mine the same, it's the law.'

'It is not the law.'

'Tis, law of ships and boats and wrecks all in, it's the law.'

'You're full of it, you are. Anyway, I didn't think there was
much about you that involved the law.'

Kel smiled again, the girl had her, Rose was good at arguing
a point down to flat flint and she liked that. She supposed
that maybe in another world where they were equal that

might have meant something, but not in this one, where past cards had been dealt and Kel's hand was full of bad odds and low numbers.

She ate the last cut of peach and they took it in turns to sip the juice from the can until the last drop had been tipped.

'Spose we should get goin,' said Kel. 'Don't like leavin the boat out there just in case.'

'In case of what?'

'I dunno, a storm or somethin.'

'Could you try and stop worrying for one night,' asked Rose. 'That would be something, wouldn't it? There's blankets over there, it isn't so bad.'

Kel took her notebook from her pocket and read over her plan it looked so simple written down.

'Here we go again,' said Rose. 'Please tell me what's in your notebook, Kel.'

'Why should I? It's private.'

Rose shrugged. 'A bit of entertainment if nothing else, I'm surprised you can write.'

Kel ignored her and turned to a new page.

'So what are you writing? Shopping list?'

Kel found a pencil in her bag and wrote PLAN 2 big and bold at the top of the page and underlined it three times.

'Pint of milk,' continued Rose, 'loaf of bread, girl, boat, new heart.'

'Shut it would you? I'm tryin to think.'

'Well good luck on that score.'

Kel sighed and she returned the pad and pencil to her bag.

She stubbed out her cigarette and got up and she supposed it wouldn't hurt for one night so she said as much. One night to write her new plan from scratch and then first light they would push on, return to the docks no matter how long it took.

'I should go check the dinghy,' said Kel. She also wanted to get the gun, it had been a bad idea to leave it.

'For what?'

'Check the rope's secure, tighten it twice.'

'I secured it already.'

Kel stood beneath the hatch and she asked the girl what it mattered to her whether she went to check the rope again or not.

'Go on then, whatever.'

Kel shook her head.

'And don't do a runner,' said Rose.

'Course not, you got all the food int you.'

'True, and I've got your baby too if you're bothered.'

Kel shrugged indifference and she looked up at the wall of stairs toward the opening. She looked at it a long time.

'What's wrong?' asked Rose.

'The hatch.'

'What about it?'

'Look at it.'

Rose came and stood beside her and they both stared up at the underside of the hatch.

'It's closed,' whispered Rose and then she said it again and asked Kel if she had shut it behind her.

Kel shook her head.

'Maybe it shut on its own?'

'How could it? Was lyin flat to the deck.'

Kel leaned against the wall and she looked at Rose and put a finger to her own lips.

'We're not alone are we?' said the girl.

Kel shook her head. 'No,' she whispered. 'We int.'

Chapter Seven

'I knew this would happen,' came a voice from somewhere above their heads. 'First the storms and risin tides and then the rebellion and then you know for defo a gang of gumbo kids gonna come round rootin.'

Kel pulled up a stool and she stood on it so she could hear clearly what the man had to say.

'We int no gang,' she shouted. 'And we int child pirates neither if that's what you're thinkin.' She heard the man stomp and haul himself about the deck and waited for a reply and when nothing came she shouted again that they were not a gang and she remembered to say something about trust.

'Where you sittin?' he asked.

'On the stools,' said Kel and she sat down.

'Move them stools back and sit on the floor.'

'We'd better do as he says,' said Rose.

Kel moved the stools and they sat with hands crossed and waited.

'You sittin?' asked the man. 'You sittin with nothin plannin down there?' His voice was shaking.

'Yes,' they both shouted in unison.

'What do you think he's going to do with us?' whispered Rose. 'He doesn't sound right, not right in the head.'

Kel watched her put a finger into the baby's mouth to keep him quiet. 'Spose he don't know *we're* all right,' she said.

'All right is you?' Suddenly the hatch flipped back and a man turned all ways toward old except his age hung head-ways through the trap like it was caught in a noose. 'Answer me!' he shouted.

'We just stopped to see what was what,' said Rose. 'We thought you might be in need of some kind of help, perhaps.'

They watched the man's eyes slip between them and Kel wished more than ever she had brought the gun from out the dinghy.

'You helped me eat my food, I see that much.'

'Just some pasta,' said Kel and she could feel the little scraping of patience she was tending flake away completely. 'Dint think it was nobody's seein there werent nobody here to claim it.'

'Here now, int I?'

Kel shrugged and said something about the law of boats and Rose kicked her.

'Where you from?' he asked.

'Cornwall same as you, sounds like.'

'You see it?'

'See what?' asked Kel.

'What you mean *what*? The end of civilisation.'

Kel went to stand and he told her to stay put.

'There's always bin riots,' said Kel.

'Not like what I seen from the harbour few days back, police couldn't hold em, it's World War Three just about. So I did a runner and came out here.'

'What you mean?' asked Rose.

'Everyone shootin everyone else.'

'Swamp folk, just?' Kel wanted to know.

'And the tower folk, some towers even got breached, that's why all the fires.'

Kel looked at Rose and said it was probably just the usual swamp uprising and then the repression that came after.

'We seen it afterwards,' she said to the man.

'What you see?' he asked. 'What you see exactly?'

'Fires on the headland, smoke all over …'

'And the people? Dead was they?'

'Some was, and more was headin that way.'

The old man nodded as if he knew it was going to happen, he'd seen it in a vision or in his dreams.

'Spose you think you're the lucky ones,' he said, head still dangling.

Kel shrugged.

'Well you int, I can tell you that right now, way things is goin you're gonna wish you were flat-backed and bloated out in the soup same as everyone. Sea's gettin worse, looters everywhere.'

Rose looked at Kel and she looked away.

'We'll see,' said Kel and she said to the man that she was going to boil a pan of water for tea.

'You mouthin me, girl?'

'I int mouthin you, sir and I can make a promise on that, just all this talkin got me thirsty is all.'

Kel waited for the man to go one of two ways, plain mental-mad or simple-smiling like they were old friends. She heard Rose hold her breath beside her.

'See you got a fire goin,' said the man. 'Spose a cup of tea int gonna hurt nobody seein you got a fire goin. I int had the smarts to do that, since the old girl rolled over and the stove went wall-ways.'

Kel nodded and she got up to fill a pan with water and she put it to boil over the rack that sat square to the metal bucket fire.

She heard Rose ask the man if he was coming down to sit, her voice a little softer, friendlier. He replied with a no and he told her that no offence was meant but he didn't trust anyone except his dog and his dog was dead.

'Don't even trust me own daughter if truth be known.'

'No offence taken,' said Rose. 'I don't trust anyone either and that includes the girl sitting next to me.'

Kel looked at Rose and noticed that a little spark had returned to her eyes, she liked that.

When the water was good enough boiling Kel added a teabag from the tin Rose had found and she simmered it dark and poured it into three metal mugs.

'You got sugar?' she asked the man.

'Nope,' he shouted from his perch. 'Bad for you.'

'No it int,' said Kel, 'it's energy and energy's good.' She passed Rose her mug and stretched up to the man to pass him his and he thanked her despite it being his tea that was being served on his boat and he told her to sit down on the floor and then told Rose to do the same.

'So,' he said, 'you kids gonna tell me how you ended up where you int sposed?'

'What you mean?' asked Kel.

'Me boat, how you happen on me boat?'

'Well,' Kel began, 'fact that it was tipped sideways and all busted out had somethin to do with it.'

'Still me boat.'

'But we dint know that did we? We did call out and everythin, spose you weren't in.'

'That's cus I was out fishin.' He spat long into the well of the cabin.

'So you've got two boats have you?' asked Rose. 'That's handy I imagine.'

'Int nothin handy bout it, most trawlers have a dinghy, it's called preparation.' Everyone was talking like it was normal everyday to sit about chatting on a sinking trawler in the middle of the ocean but truth was the old man had them captive and Kel didn't like that one bit.

'I've bin livin on this ere boat roundabout my whole life, she int so big but she's my life. I knew it would happen, just dint know when.' He dangled his legs through the hatch and

Kel thought how easy it would be to grab one of those legs and pull him to the ground. She was losing patience, had started to wonder if he'd found the dinghy, worse, if he had found the gun.

'Spose you wonder what happened to the old girl.' He patted the boat in case they didn't know what he was talking about.

'So what did happen?' asked Rose.

'The truth is if I knew I'd tell you but I don't so I won't.'

The two intruders looked at each other and shrugged.

'One minute I was at the docks and the next I was headin out as fast as I could go, boat must have hit somethin and before I knew it I got tipped and knocked myself clean out with the winch.'

'Rocks do you reckon?' asked Rose.

'I dunno, I came out into the Channel to get away from Falmouth, never used to be rocks out here, but I keep seein things that weren't there before, land and then no land. Dunno, maybe another boat got me, but then where's the boat?'

'Maybe a ship,' said Kel. 'Maybe that's it.'

'Maybe, there's bin a fair share of traffic recent what with everythin, vessels all over with folks unable to make land.'

Kel moved herself from the floor and on to a stool and she asked the old man what he knew to distract him from noticing.

'Same as you, the shootin and the runnin and then the fires, you seen em, they was everywhere. I just headed south, but now I don't know where I am.'

Kel shook her head and said they only saw a few fires and the aftermath and that was all.

Rose copied Kel and helped herself to a stool. 'Do you ... do you know which towers went down?'

'Wait a minute,' said Kel. 'We don't know that any came down for certain, give em all a few days and things will be back to normal.'

'Dint see much in truth,' said the man. 'I was lucky, was still out in the harbour, bin fishin for mackerel. Heard it more un saw it and when I looked up the sky was full of fire, fallin fire, like stars but mad close. Fires rained down on all and every one. Made a change from water at least.'

'So you dint see no towers come down?'

'I know what I heard.'

'What do you reckon?' Rose asked Kel.

'Probably just lootin got out of hand, you know what folks is like, if you can't have it burn it.'

'Is that right?' Rose looked at her and raised an eyebrow and Kel looked away and she wished she had a way with words that was settling but instead she looked at the man and asked him straight if they were hostages because she felt like they were.

He laughed. 'You int no hostages.'

'So we can head out then, if we want.'

The old man ignored her and he told them he'd known something bad was going to happen. 'Somethin in the air, way the fog tasted on me tongue and the movement of the

108

tides, they was all wrong. Kept seein things then not seein em.' Then he asked if they had felt the water.

'What water?' asked Rose.

'Seawater, you felt it?'

Kel nodded, she had wondered about it every time she put her hands into the water to soothe her blisters.

'It's warm,' he continued. 'Tepid, now you tell me why the ocean's gone tepid.'

'No idea,' said Kel and she leaned forward to see if she could spot the gun. She could feel her patience slipping. 'You gonna let us go?' she asked.

'Spose things have changed forever now,' he continued and he looked down below deck toward the baby that slept against Rose's back and then he caught Kel's eye, 'but if you wanna go then go. I int stoppin you.'

Kel glanced at Rose and saw that she was looking back with a face that pleaded with her to stay one night.

'No,' Kel whispered.

'But he looks sad,' said Rose.

'All the more reason to get gone.'

'Sad and lonely.'

'Sad and crazy.'

'You kids got a fancy for crackers?' the man asked and he let himself fall into the hatch. 'I got a fancy for crackers.' He picked himself up off the floor and went limping toward the back of the upturned cupboards to rummage.

'Couldn't we just stay one night?' asked Rose. 'He's got blankets and don't forget the food.'

Kel wanted to say that she was planning to take the food with them anyway, maybe even the blankets. She looked at the man and stood suddenly, her heart stopped in her mouth. 'Hey, that's my gun,' she shouted.

'What this?' He swung the rifle that was on a strap around his shoulder. 'Tis mine now.'

'Don't reckon.'

He held the gun lightly in his hands and told her to sit back down and reluctantly she did.

'So just you two is it?' he asked. 'And that baby of yours.'

Kel nodded, obviously.

'All alone on the big blue?'

'We've got each other,'said Kel, 'We're fine.'

'Looks like you could do with another pair of hands, help you row or whatever.'

'We're good thanks.'

'Is that right.'

'How big's your dinghy?' Kel asked. 'Maybe you could live on that for a while?'

'Bout same as yours I'd say.'

'Tiny then?'

The old man shrugged.

'Why don't you pack up and set off same as us, take your chances, leave this boat behind.'

'Where you goin?' he asked.

'Dunno yet.' Kel looked at Rose for the shut-up. 'What about you? Where were you goin before you crashed?'

'I was headin Land's End.'

'You plannin on stoppin there?'

'No chance, there's nowhere to land the boat, I was hopin to swing around the headland and back up the north coast.

'It's the lack of company that gets me down,' he continued, 'since me dog passed and all.' He looked at Rose and smiled and Kel knew it was because he sensed weakness there. Then he laughed and offered up the crackers.

'What about your daughter?' asked Rose. 'Maybe you could pay her a visit?'

'Me daughter? I int spendin more time than I have to with her, spanner short of a tool bag that one, despite only being a teen.'

'Time to go anyway,' said Kel. 'If we int hostages.' She stood and looked at Rose to do the same.

'Company's everythin though innit?' he said, as if he hadn't heard. 'Now the world's gone imploded, it's kind of the end I reckon?'

Kel ignored him and she thanked him for his hospitality and added that if it was any consolation she didn't think the world had blown away with bedlam, except perhaps Cornwall, and even then it was only the part they had seen. And maybe the fires would have dried the juice out of the swamp earth just a little.

'Two young girls out there on their own. You can take care of this one can you, plus the baby?'

Kel was already at the hatch when she realised the man had placed himself between them and was asking Rose a question.

'I reckon she can just as well look after herself,' Kel said. 'Bein a girl's the same as bein a boy or a man or a woman. Now what's it gonna take to get you to part with some food?'

The man look down at his hands. 'This gun,' he said coldly. 'This gun and all the ammo you got stashed.'

Kel nodded the deal done, she preferred knife protection in any case. They filled a plastic sack with unopened packets of rice and pasta and carried it to the boat whilst the man looked on and Kel thought how pathetic he looked, the gun in his hands and not once did he think to use it to chase them from the boat. He could have kept everything, except the one thing he wanted, company.

'You're not so nice are you,' said Rose as Kel took up the oars.

'He was a weirdo,' said Kel.

'He weren't weird, just lonely is all.' Rose unwound the baby from its binding when it started to shout hunger and passed it to Kel and Kel turned to feed it and then returned it to the centre of the boat.

'He had weirdo elements sparkin all ways inside him,' continued Kel. 'He was odd, had his eyes up and down you like paint stripper.'

'No he didn't. What happened to you to make you so damaged?'

'What you mean?'

'You think everyone's about to bite or burn you.'

'Life,' said Kel. 'Life's what happened to me.' She looked

at Rose through the coming light of dawn and shrugged. It was life and everything in it that meant existing.

When morning crept up on them it wore a shroud of heavy-weight fog. It filled the boat like rolling-rock gravel and it stuffed their hearts the same. They sat with big bags of misery lying low in their chests and Kel watched Rose for sparks and Rose watched Kel the same. Their happening upon the trawler and the food and company besides had entertained them and distracted them into complacency, but now they were back in the boat the reality came crashing back. And now they were gunless.

'What now?' asked Rose and she said she knew Kel had a plan but maybe she had forgotten it.

'We keep goin the way we bin goin,' she said. 'To the end of the Channel and up around to the north coast.'

'You sure?'

'Positive, we're not far from land. If it wasn't for these stupid oars we'd be home and dry by now.'

'OK,' said Rose, 'if you say so.'

Kel sat forward and looked at Rose. It was as if the girl was waiting for her to fail. 'I seen the stars last night, just got to keep goin forward.'

'Isn't everywhere forward?'

Kel ignored her. Instead she emptied the last of the collected water into her bottle and drank and then she passed the bottle to Rose.

'I'm not thirsty,' Rose said. 'Just had tea.'

'You need to keep drinkin in any case.'

Rose lifted the bottle to her lips and took a small sip. 'Tastes like plastic.'

'That's cus it's off the creases in the boat and the raincoat mostly.' She wished she'd remembered to barter water.

'It won't kill us will it?'

'Course not. Anyway, it's more or less what you've been drinkin last two days straight – where you think I was gettin the water topped up from?'

Kel knelt to check the lines for a possible catch and she was careful to pass it from hand to hand so as not to scare the fish.

'Anything?' asked Rose.

'Nothin.'

'It'd be nice to have something fresh for breakfast. We can't eat the rice or the pasta until we can light a fire.'

'Least we're full, for now.' Kel continued to reel in the line she had threaded through her fingers and she rested her stomach on the side of the boat and looked deep into the grey-green churn of ocean. It really was quite warm, now she thought of it.

With the arrival of the fog a new wet cold had come into the air and it pricked their skin goosey and pinned them rigid to the boat. The weather had angles and shadows pushed through it that weren't there before and Kel worried that it had changed for good. She could see the waves moving all around them and felt their curl in her gut as they grappled for the hold beneath the dinghy.

The idea of drowning came to her suddenly and it was both ridiculous and realistic. It could happen and in all honesty would happen, but until that moment the horror of suffocating in water was so huge she was unable to think about it head on. Kel sat back into the dip of boat and she pulled her jacket from out of her bag and put it around her shoulders and she placed the rain mac across the baby.

'Don't like this fog,' said Rose. 'Don't like it one bit.'

'What int to like bout ridin the ocean and all time your own?'

Rose tried to laugh but Kel knew she was feeling it. After the trawler and basic eating and walking around like normal the girl was feeling it. The fog was in her and Kel knew this well enough because it was in her too.

Kel offered more water and checked the last of the lines and she wished she could say something to make light of the situation to keep them from it, but there was nothing to say and nothing to do but wait for the fog to lift and the day to pass and a bright starry night to strike out so they could get back on course.

'Are you sure we're heading in the right direction?' asked Rose.

'I'm sure enough.' said Kel.

'It's cold isn't it.'

Kel nodded.

'Damn cold like winter,' Rose continued. Cold and fog and god knows what. Did I tell you I get claustrophobi

'No but that's fine out here innit?'

'Not really, the fog's the worst of it, I can't see anything but an orange rubber ring and you just about.'

'That's somethin then.'

'I hate orange. Why can't they make these rubber boats pink?'

'I'd say most fisherfolk int into pink.'

'I really don't like this at all.'

Kel looked at the girl and the fear that flashed there and she told Rose to look at her. 'If you look at me you'll see I'm fine and then you'll know that things are fine.'

Rose pushed forward to the centre of the boat and Kel could see her eyes stretched wide with the miasma cloud pressed to them and she told her that things would turn out right and for once the girl did not argue.

When Rose asked her to tell something from her past that might resemble story Kel had to think hard and she rummaged through everything that was etched there and she told the girl that she had nothing of any worth.

'You must have something,' said Rose. 'For all your wild living and whatever else.'

Kel shook her head.

'Please, give me something to take my mind off this.'

scratched her head to put thinking into it and she
mind to the swamps and her father's shack but
ntertainment there.

childhood?' asked Rose.

sea and she wished she had the nerve to

say truthfully what weight swung there but the girl was looking for some kind of cheery.

'Can't remember,' she said.

'You can't remember your childhood?'

Kel shrugged and she looked at the girl and a part of her hoped Rose saw the pain and confusion that was in her so she would not have to explain the intricacies of a life lived on the edge and slipping.

When the baby made like it was about to cry they moved forward and the distraction was welcomed.

'Might not come to much,' said Kel finally. 'The storm or whatever might just blow out or past and we might just be thinkin on somethin too much.' Kel said this, but she wasn't sure what she believed. The waves were getting higher, she could see the white caps of foam as they broke against each other and joined forces turning toward the boat. Each wave that hit them bigger than the one before, faster.

She peered beyond the waves. Out there somewhere were rays of light and at some point they would fan and pool into the boat and show them the way, she told herself to believe this and she believed it enough to settle her own nerves. Their fate had just got muddled in the shroud a moment, somewhere in the dull grey fudge of patient waiting.

But when she closed her eyes momentarily and put her nose to the wind she recognised the heady earthen tang of autumn rain journeying across the ocean and she knew it was pitching their way. She looked at the girl and saw withou doubt that damaging dread had set in and she picked up bubbling baby and held it to her and she told the girl to lie down and get some rest and that was what Rose did.

'I'm goin to anchor down, we int goin nowhere tonight.'

Kel settled the baby in her lap and reached for the anchor that hung from the back of the boat and was careful to unwind the rope and let it sink into the sea. She sat back and hid the baby from the wind and when the rain came hammering she hooked the raincoat over its head and tented it to shelter. The storm could try its best and worst and they would pretend all was well and good-time coming.

If Kel could just hold the baby down to sleep then she might sleep the same, tumble partway toward calm and fill the empty void with the promise that everything would be OK. To briefly hide was to loop a little hope up close and closing, zip the water world from her eyes and all things she should have known as threat and everything she should have seen coming.

They were not alone on the ocean in any case. When sleep for resting's sake refused to come Kel lay with her head turned sea-surf looking.

At first the tiny blot on the horizon was just that, a blot and a smudge of large looping wave and Kel made a note of it and marked it as nothing worth bothering and instead she ᴅd the water world snake and coil into a vortex where ᴇnt they might fall. Everything the same and hen her eyes stumbled back upon the blot k-stain crawling toward them.

le and she blinked and blinked again and

she rubbed the rain from her face so she might see the thing on the horizon: it was a boat and it was heading straight for them.

'Rose,' she shouted. 'Rose we're gonna be rescued.'

Kel stood and waited for the vessel to get closer but it happened so fast she didn't see the winch until too late, didn't have time to jump out of its way and its weight hit fully against her forehead and knocked her clean out.

Chapter Eight

Whatever was and whatever wasn't everything moved in a blur of colourless comings and goings. Kel lay huddled some-where in the forever dark of ocean night and occasionally she made out the rhythm of sentences as they scattered like broken glass around her but nothing made any kind of sense. She had been swinging in and out of consciousness for what seemed like hours, the pitch black of the room she was in made it impossible to determine the time of day or night.

Voices on the deck above her head were kept low and ⸳ded, whispered words chewed and spat into the wind, we⸳⸳ ⸳ng.

Kel ⸳⸳⸳ feel pain pulsing in her head and she put a hand ⸳⸳ it to feel ⸳⸳ bump of bruise rising from her skull above ⸳ eye.

⸳⸳ had no ⸳⸳⸳llection of how she came to be on this ⸳⸳⸳ knew it was not the crazy old man's vessel ⸳⸳⸳eel it steaming forward. She remembered the crane and the swinging chain that hit the back of her head and guessed she had been knocked out, by hand or by accident she didn't know or best case she had passed out. She tried to untangle her wrists from the itching rope that bound them and when for the hundredth time she failed then anger took hold and she shouted out Rose's name and heard nothing but laughter returned.

Kel wondered where Rose and the baby were, wondered where they'd been hidden or put and she held back from thinking the worst. She sat up and kicked into the black until her toes touched the side of the room and she moved best she could toward the iron wall so she would have something to lean against. The room's smell was akin to alcohol spilt and dried and spilt again. A room that was meant for storing and preserving fish but which had long since been retired, she guessed. The rancid scent spun Kel further into thinking on things that might or might not have been there.

She put her head back against the cold steel to make something of where she was and what she might do to escape but nothing came to mind and she knew nothing would. She had been defeated and she knew from experience that there would be no way back from the thing. If somebody had got the upper hand enough to knock the spark out of her there wasn't much left to be done except wait.

The ocean had become a dangerous place, same as the mainland just about; a place where once perhaps a handshake ruled had now become a realm without rules complete. The water world was run by pirates and Kel knew this well enough, even before the door opened and the light lit up her face and in passing flagged up the crates of bootleg at the room's far end.

She looked into the oil-lamp light and at the kid that held it and she knew the kid was waiting for her to speak and Kel waited the same.

'You're awake,' said the lamp-bearer suddenly. 'Now maybe you can tell us who you are, where you're goin.'

Kel's head swam with pain but she tried to hide it with anger, bravado built from shame. 'What's happened?' she asked. 'Who the hell are you?'

'This int to do with me.' The boy walked around her, came close and crouched. 'I'm just doin what the majority voted for. You need to tell me who you are.'

'I int nobody.' Kel straightened her back against the wall.

'Don't lie, the others won't like that.'

'Lie about what?' Kel felt the salt-blisters on her lips unstick and rip and seep liquid.

'You're keepin stuff from us, that other girl's the same and don't say you int cus you is.'

Kel sat forward and her head felt too heavy to hold, she felt it teetering upon her neck. 'Rose,' she said.

'That's her name, we know that much about her.'

'Nobody bin askin me nothin,' she whispered. 'I int seen nobody.' She thought things back and she thought things forward from when they had been sailing in the dinghy and she had no recollection other than sitting in the dinghy, settling to the storm, followed by the crane hitting her unconscious.

122

'So you tellin me there int nothin in you? You just so happen to be out snoopin the high seas just cus?' The boy pushed closer and he filled the space that wasn't crammed with crates and boxes of contraband.

'Snoopin where, what's there to snoop about?' Kel put her hands to her head to hold it but the rope that bound them bit too tight and she returned them to her lap.

'The old man said you was snoopin, takin what int yours.'

Kel shook her head and she tried to see the boy's face and she told him they had only taken food from him in exchange for a gun, that it was a fair and square exchange.

The boy laughed and he asked Kel if the gun he was holding was the gun she was talking about.

Kel nodded and said yes, that was it.

'Expensive piece of weaponry innit?' The boy smiled.

'Spose, dunno.'

'Spose you int gonna tell me where you got it from.'

'Can't remember,' Kel lied. She was getting impatient despite the banging in her head.

'That's a shame,' he said. 'We could do with more of these is all.' He sat down on the floor and placed the lamp beside him.

'Well I could do with more food,' said Kel, and she added that food was worth more to her than any guns.

'Is that right?'

'Since whatever it was that kicked off is right.' She wiggled forward to test if the boy was in kicking distance, almost.

'Just the usual chaos,' he laughed and stepped back, 'Nothin worse than usual anyway. It works for us.'

123

'Who's us?'

'You'll see.'

Kel relaxed a little because the boy didn't have much of the scare about him, he was physically smaller than her, perhaps the same age but he didn't look like a fighter, he smiled too much and Kel marked his friendliness as his biggest weakness. The more he talked, the more he might think he could trust her, become an ally. She asked what had sparked things this time.

'Damn if I know, I int bin on the mainland since forever.'

'Land int worth much in any case, mostly swamp land,' said Kel.

'That's why we're out here skatin in the pond. Some of us bin out here a year.'

'You pirates?' Kel asked. 'You loot and all the rest?'

The boy nodded.

She thought maybe him and her were getting on OK and so she asked him if he could untie her for the stretch but the answer was no. She asked about Rose and was told she was fine.

'Her baby's fine too.' He picked up the gun that sat in his lap and pretended to clean it. 'So how you find yourself in a boat with a tower girl?'

'Tower girl? Thought you said she int worth nothin.'

'It's not hard to tell the difference between a girl from the towers and a girl from the swamps.'

'Circumstance,' sighed Kel. 'Whatever this is, whatever

you want with me, you can let her go. She int the type of girl
to be locked up or whatever.'

'Know that.'

'She int the type to be treated mean neither.'

'Not like you then.'

'Not like me or you or that gang of stompin, laughin kids
I hear bangin above deck.'

The boy leaned forward. 'Never mind bout them.'

'I int, but I'm mindin em on the girl's behalf.'

The boy put down the gun and returned the lamp into his
hands, paused for a minute and Kel thought perhaps he was
going to offer her a way out.

'So this girl, friend of yours is she?' he asked.

Kel thought for a minute. 'Kind of.'

'Best buddy friends?'

'No.'

'Just friends then?'

Kel shrugged and said yes, she was a friend.

'Int so alike though is you?'

'So?' Kel didn't know where things were travelling and her
head spun out in confusion.

'So you met up just as then? Out on a river laneway or
whatever?'

'What you gettin at?'

'She int like you is what I'm gettin at. I int sure you two
got all that much in common at all.'

Kel knew what he was getting at, but she let him carry on
running his mouth off in any case.

'Seems to me you bumped into that girl accidentally on purpose and you're bringin her somewhere or someplace close to payday.'

Kel thought for a moment, she didn't want to give anything of herself or her plans away.

'Cus she's rich int she and you int,' he continued, 'and when things calm down on the mainland like they usually do that girl will be worth somethin.' He stood and stepped back, held the light to his face. 'See what I'm gettin at here? So you tell me her name and why you've got her and things will sort themselves out just fine.'

'Where you got her put?' Kel was getting angry, tried again to twist free of her restraints.

'Away some. She's fine, won't be long now anyway.'

'What won't be?'

'Gettin to where we're goin.'

'Where we goin?'

The boy laughed and he got up and said as if he would tell her, and when Kel asked him for his name at least he laughed twice and left the room.

Kel hooked her eyes back into the black inkwell that was the burrow below deck and listened to the tussle of jubilant, fighting kids up above who knew they had struck gold with the find that was Rose. Kel knew they wouldn't stop with the riffling and ripping until they found out the exact details of Kel's plan. It was obvious that she and Rose were not friends or from the same place and once they took a good look at the gun they would put two and two together.

The girl had the look of money about her: it wouldn't be long until they wondered about that gun and worked out that Rose was the daughter of an arms dealer.

Kel knew it wouldn't be long before they extracted the truth.

She reached for her canteen the best she could with the rope choking and cutting where it touched limb-skin and she drank the warm swill water that it had been filled with and it tasted of all the things it shouldn't have. Kel thought about the pirate boy and when she felt the engine buck and heard the anchor chain clink and fall she knew she had all the anger she needed for the fight ahead.

She waited for the engine to stop completely and listened out for the sounds of the docks perhaps returned to normal but there were none. Nothing but the waves coming good against the hull of the boat and the shouts of kids above board and the shouts of kids out there somewhere on unreconisable land.

Kel kept her eye on where she had last seen the door open and waited for it to open and she didn't have to wait long.

'So you're the swamper who swapped the gun for food,' shouted a girl. 'The one who int botherin to say much at all.'

Kel watched the girl step into the square of artificial light and stand against the door jamb, a can of beer in her hand.

'Well?' the girl asked.

'Well what?'

'Who the hell are you and more importantly, who's the pretty posh girl?' She took a slurp of her drink.

127

Kel didn't like this girl, she looked weak, like somebody who was used to telling others what to do. They had a name for girls like that in the swamps, she was a maggoty bully.

'And where did you get the gun? Don't say my dad, I know that bit. Least he had smarts enough to get it off you I spose. Still, he's an idiot.' She entered the room fully and put the lamp she was carrying on to one of the crates.

'Why's that?' asked Kel.

'Why's what?'

'Why's your dad an idiot?'

'Dint I just say? He let you go.'

Kel decided the old man was right, this kid had a crazy streak running right through her.

'You took the gun off him,' she said. 'I did a deal with him, not you.'

The girl stood up and threw the can of beer at Kel. It missed and hit the wall in a fizz.

'The gun, where you get it?' the maggot girl shouted.

'Found it,' Kel said.

'Folk don't leave guns like that lyin around, it's a bloody machine gun.'

Kel kept quiet.

'So now, what you got to say for yourself?'

Kel shrugged, it had been a long day night day and night again, she knew staying quiet was the only option available to her; about the girl, about the gun, about anything.

'You got a word suckin anywhere there inside your gob?'

'Got plenty words for a girl like you. Which one you want?' The kid was a bully and Kel didn't like her. She wasn't scared either.

'Where you find the gun?' The girl came close and pulled Kel to her feet.

'On a ship,' said Kel.

'Which ship?' The girl jabbed two fingers into Kel's stomach for the sake of intimidation but it didn't work.

'No idea.' Kel stood best she could with everything tied and she promised herself that she would not tell on the tower girl who was hers for the groundwork that had been completed.

'And how you know the posh girl, found her the same did you?'

'I already told that boy, we're friends.' Kel felt a bit of her old self come back to her, the bit that was flapping Crow beast. 'Good friends,' she lied.

'Bull,' shouted the girl.

'How you know?'

'Cus I bin speakin to her.'

'And what she tell you?' Kel swallowed hard, she realised her safety depended on what the girl had said, the girl *she* had kidnapped.

'She tells me you int no friends. Don't take a genius to work that out, anyhow.'

'You're lyin,' said Kel.

'Am I now? The girl pushed into her and Kel could smell the stale alcohol on her breath.

'A stinkin liar,' Kel continued. 'In fact, you don't look like you got much in you at all cept bullyin.'

'What's that sposed to mean?'

'Means what's meant.'

'You ribbin me?'

Kel sucked at her teeth to indicate she was thinking. 'Spose,' she said at last. 'Just a bit.' Kel had a feeling the girl was going to prove herself one way or the other and she was right.

The girl punched her once in her stomach and once in her face and Kel spat the blood on to the floor in defiance.

'You want more?' the girl asked and Kel shook her head and said that no she didn't want more but if the girl thought she held all the cards now she was wrong and not just bit-wrong but double wrong.

The girl didn't know what to say and Kel thought maybe she hadn't heard her right with all the swagger that burst from her and the mental madness that went with that and so Kel waited for the next shot but it didn't come.

Instead the girl made a thing of blindfolding Kel. Then she grabbed her by the knot around her wrists and pulled her from the hull and out on to the deck. Kel stood to take in her surroundings through her nose and mouth and she could sense by the taste and tang of the air that it was still night and she took comfort in that. She was more of the night when bad came biting and she could make more of scheming in the dark.

Obediently she followed the girl dragging her as they stepped from the boat and soon the hands of other pirate kids came poking and pushing to put some scent-claim on her. Dogs marking their territory, that was what they were: mongrels making something out of their existence that was better than nothing.

Kel went on stumbling and following as told. She knew there were rocks beneath her feet for the slip and cut but still she went on because the kids told her to. She asked to have the rope loosened at her feet and was ignored but when the blindfold loosened around her face Kel shook her head to let it drop around her neck. In the dark nobody seemed to notice.

Kel took her time to take in her new surroundings. She had thought perhaps they were on the mainland, wished it were so, but when she saw the lighthouse rise up in front of her the little bit of last-ditch hope shrunk inside.

'Pirate base,' she said to herself.

Her words made the kids laugh, some of them cheered because in their minds they were in heaven. They lived by their own rules, had nobody to teach them right from wrong and if Kel didn't have her sights set on America and her operation she might have thought it perfect too.

They pushed her into the lighthouse and she saw its single winding staircase spiralling upwards, but instead they kept pushing her down, down more steps until she reached the very bottom deep in the rock and she fell into an empty room, her knees hitting concrete as the door locked behind her.

Kel sat up and with her hands still tied she mopped the

blood that ran from her cheek with the blindfold. She called out to Rose and heard the faint return of her own name from another room higher up in the lighthouse and she took joy from that one brief second moment. The thread that stitched between still tied them and that was worth something, even when the girl with the mental red flag waving within returned to kick Kel unconscious.

Another day or week could have come around counting and Kel wouldn't have known anything of the fractal world outside. The strange and the strangers beyond the lock-down door and the granite bricks that went around. When she called out Rose's name this time nothing but seagulls called back. She was alone again.

Kel noticed her canteen had been refilled and thrown to her sometime during the knock-out phase and Kel guessed the boy that was OK had been and gone. She drank some and washed the blood best she could from off her hands and knees and face and she sat cold and close with the memory of a bad life behind her and the thought that her life ahead was just about the same.

Kel propped herself against the wall and supped a little more of the water. The cold of night was everywhere in her. She knew no bones were broken because things that could move did, but when she held still everything inside her felt bust and twisted and set wrong.

The lighthouse was a shaking bottle and she the dreg-end swirling in the bottom. The thought of a little camp settled out here in the middle of the sea was so strange. It struck Kel as the craziest thing and if she'd had less ache in her bones she would have laughed out loud for the bizarre notion that was the child pirate base.

She studied the one wall that coiled around and around and around. She looked at the door and wondered about its thickness and the lock that twisted against her on the other side. There was nothing in the room besides but despite its wash of white Kel felt the creep of dark-matter memory all around her. She could see it and smell it and it was soaked through with the stench of home.

Kel drew her knees up close to her chest and she crossed her arms to hugging. She tried to think of some tune, the way her older sisters used to tell her to do. To find some happy and hold on to it no matter what. She closed her eyes and tried to focus, snatching at things that were supposed to be gift-good for settling the want to scream.

Nothing came.

The night was a long night and it didn't give much of itself except the light bulb that glared down on Kel. She watched it for flies, but knew she was the only living thing in that room and she took up her canteen and hurled it hard and it smashed the thing dead where it dangled.

Kel watched the worm-red filament wiggle and fizz the last of its fire and when it burnt itself out complete she let the memory of light fade with it and the dark that had been prodding at her finally push in.

All through the night she let the dark have its way and it was a long night stripped of all image except eyes. Dad's eyes, her eyes.

When morning came Kel was waiting for it. She knew by the slip of boots running the stairs and the bang of doors that replaced the rhythmic, savage sea that the rowdy kids were up and doing.

She stood at the door and tried every crack and corner for looking and when she heard footsteps scuffing the stairs down to her she sat backed-up on the ground and waited. She hoped it was the boy and it was.

'Got you food,' he declared as he kicked the door wide. 'Got you lobster.' He laughed because lobster for breakfast was ridiculous. 'We all had it. Int poison, is what I'm sayin.'

He asked Kel to sit back whilst he placed the tin plate central to the room and then retreated to the door.

'I won't bite,' said Kel as she crouched to the food. 'Know you're just followin orders, but still.'

'I int followin no orders but my own.'

Kel picked the meat from the claws and ate it and it was good and she fingered more into her mouth and the boy watched. When she was finished she said she thought the little maggot girl was in charge and the boy laughed.

'No,' he shouted. 'She just thinks she is and it keeps her quiet to think it.'

'So who is?'

134

'We all are, it's a democracy.' He crouched in front of Kel to cut the rope at her feet and told her that was why he was looking after her.

'Why?' she asked.

'Maybe we can do a deal.'

'For me and Rose?'

'Just you.'

Kel thought for a minute. Had this boy finally figured out who Rose was? Had she told them?

'Join us,' he continued. 'You'll get to be a part of our gang. Join us.'

'Why this big offer all of a sudden, what's Rose said to you?'

'Nothin much, not yet, anyway.'

This surprised Kel.

'God knows why, it's obvious she int no drug-runner like you.'

Kel flinched. She didn't like to hear what she was out loud. 'How you know I'm a runner?' she asked.

'I seen you roundabout the swamps, before I joined pirates. I knew your face was familiar. Crow, int you? You can tell me, I'm a swamp kid too.'

Kel shook her head.

The boy sensed Kel's discomfort. 'Don't mean to dis you or nothin, Crows are a big deal in the swamps. You could do better than be draggin her around on your own is all.'

'What does that mean?'

'Means maybe we could help each other out.'

Kel folded her arms and waited for him to say the thing she knew he was going to say.

'Girl like you,' he continued, 'got certain skills, int you. We could do with you on the team.'

'Team?' Kel scoffed and shook her head.

'You should think about it is all I'm sayin. We know you've got some payday comin, but let us in on it and you can be a part of somethin with us, somethin good.'

Kel looked at him and asked what it was he wanted from her.

'I want you to tell me who the girl is.'

'She int nobody.'

'You're right, she int worth it, so join us.'

Kel shook her head. The old Kel would have made a deal, but she had got to know Rose, and selfishness had been replaced with guilt. 'No,' she said.

'You got some control over her int you, or she on you?'

Kel shrugged. 'Don't reckon.'

'See I know you kidnapped her for money, or somethin better, and you're bringin her from A to B.' The boy stood up suddenly. 'I've known all along.'

Kel struggled to stand the same.

'What gets me,' he continued, 'is why she's botherin to protect you.' He said this and he said it over as he left the room and turned the key.

Kel leaned against the wall with the dizzying bricks circling left and right and she wondered why Rose kept from telling the truth. Maybe the tower girl thought it was better to know the beast that was Kel than these sea monsters. Kel thought about the baby too and wondered if it had been fed and then she stretched to the ground and moved enough to have a little life come to her. To move was to stop the what-why questions, but it didn't work. Things were happening and they were happening fast and Kel knew the kids would keep the girl and work out some way to use her to their best advantage, whether Kel told them her own plan or not.

It was only a matter of time until they sussed where the gun had come from and then they would know what the girl was worth and suddenly Kel would be of no value to them. They wouldn't want her as part of the team whether she said yes or not.

She rubbed her head, her eyes. Everything hurt and it was all made worse by the boy's words.

'Team,' she said. What kind of teamwork did a gang of pirates have to offer? Kel guessed they did the same work as she did, the difference was she worked alone. She wished she could trust someone; anyone would do, if she did she could work with them, make a new kind of family to rival the Crows, get to be at the top of her game, but the pirate kids were just that and she doubted they got much done in the way of plans, high hopes. Then she thought about Rose and felt something in her gut tighten, that guilt again. Rose had become hers for the looking after and although Kel didn't own her she owned the right to see the whole thing through. Maybe there was still a chance to set the stones of her plan back into step.

Kel put a hand to her chest, to feel her heart beat was to know it was complete, no matter that it skipped time and played its own rhythm occasionally. She went to the door and tried to imagine the stairs and how they twisted through the neck of the serpent building. She counted out the floors as she placed them in her mind's eye and there were many, a lighthouse full to bursting with delinquent kids. She wished she had thought of the idea first: a derelict bolt-hole from which to pinch and pilfer the high seas at whim and be safe in the knowledge that they were alone. She could have worked a mean business shipping goods all over from here. Still could, maybe.

'Rose,' she whispered, 'where are you?'

Kel banged at the door and called out to the boy standing guard that she was ready to talk and not just words for the sake of speaking but the truth, if that was what they wanted to hear.

'What's the racket?' he shouted through the door.

'I'll talk,' said Kel again and she waited for the key to turn and the door to open. They stood close and Kel realised for the first time that he looked much like herself and all the other kids that lived their lives cutting it in flood-plain country ditches.

'I'll talk,' she said again when he opened the door.

'What made you change your mind?' he asked.

'Bin thinkin, maybe we can come to some agreement.'

'I knew it!' The boy laughed and waved the knife that he had been playing with and Kel recognised it as her own.

'You better come with me,' he said and he pointed up the stairs and told Kel to lead on.

'You take as long as you like,' He put away the knife and gestured towards the stairs. 'We got all the time in the world.'

'How far we headin?' asked Kel.

'Last door before the top.'

'You got Rose up there?'

'Maybe.'

When they reached the right door the boy pushed past and knocked. Kel waited patiently at his shoulder and she looked on up the stairs toward the room right at the top that had one time in its life housed the warning light. The flash that once was had now been extinguished, and all that was left of the lighthouse was a length of rock that hid in the dark and clubbed all else into submission.

'What?' shouted the girl from inside the room.

The boy turned the handle and pushed open the door.

The maggot girl looked across from where she was standing at the window and it took her a moment to notice through the crowd of kids that Kel stood with the boy.

'She wants to speak,' he said and he pushed Kel into the room that housed nothing but table and chairs and the big ocean sky dazzling in the round.

'Where's the girl?' asked Kel. 'Where's Rose?'

'She's fine,' said the boss girl. 'Probably more fine than she was with you.' She told the boy to close the door behind them.

'Where's Rose?' asked Kel.

'Safe,' said the girl.

'I want to see her.'

'Int you wanna know bout the baby?'

Kel shrugged whatever and she pretended not to hear the other girls giggling behind them.

'The tower girl said he was yours.'

'Don't mean I care much, just show me Rose and I'll tell you everythin you want to know.'

'OK.' She nodded.

Kel waited. She could hear a clock tick somewhere above their heads like impatient fingers snapping attention to the room full of gang kids. They circled Kel and they circled the girl and whether it was expectation or hope holding out for some kind of battle Kel knew they would not be disappointed.

'So go on,' said the girl.

'Tell me Rose is right: shout her and get her to shout back.'

The girl started to laugh, she moved nearer and Kel tried to slow her breathing. She told herself not to get into a fight, because if she did it would be the end of her. She looked at the girl and saw the crazy coming into her eyes, with each second the clock ticked she moved closer to Kel.

Suddenly the door kicked open and a boy Kel hadn't seen before ran into the room.

'It's the tower girl,' he shouted. 'We worked out who she is.'

The maggot girl turned toward him. 'Go on.'

'That gun, it's military, stolen from the dockyard. That tower girl is the daughter of an arms dealer.'

'Bingo!' shouted the girl and everybody cheered.

Kel felt something shake and break loose inside and it was the feeling she harboured since infancy; the rattle of anger and of dread tearing and clawing for freedom. But she stood steady. With Dad anything other than quiet still meant the beat. She told herself this maggot girl was not worth the rise and to keep calm, to think about her heart, but when the girl pushed herself against her there was no reasoning left but the punch, she'd been found out. Kel knew she was out of options and she raised her best-shot hand and balled it and unleashed a huge one-two.

The girl lay on the ground and her shock mirrored Kel's own. The clock ticked on whilst the room held its breath, then every other kid in the room came for her.

She lay with her knees to her chest and her arms wrapped around her, eyes closed as always, it was best.

The beating didn't take so long that Kel had time to think about mortality. To be kicked and to be punched was just that and she was used to just that. They were all the same in any case. Every kid had the caustic metal melting inside of them; they all had an axe to grind so sparks could fly.

When the girl shouted for them to stop the other kids did what they were instructed and she told them to hurry up, bring the swamp girl down.

Kel breathed a sigh of relief. She let the boy lift her from the floor, and she didn't speak because nobody would be listening. The girl and her gang had stormed from the room and Kel was pushed to follow.

Half-shoved, half-carried down the stairs, Kel wondered if

this really was it. Death, and not just death but *slaughter* at the hands of swamp kids as good as kin. She couldn't hate them for it and she knew she would have done the same given the circumstances. Smacking those who did not comply was her thing after all. Or it had been her thing in the swamps, before Rose and the conscience the girl had unwittingly planted in her.

Kel followed the others and she wondered if one last-ditch attempt could be made to get away.

'What gets me bout folks like yourself is you think you're better cus there's a bit of business bout you when we know you're way worse.' The maggot girl was at it again.

'Why's that?' Kel asked.

'The boy told me you was an inbred Crow and we don't want your stinkin drug-runnin near us.'

Kel stopped suddenly, the anger blasted from her despite the everywhere ache and she could feel her heart rip a little. 'What you work that's different?' she asked.

'Everythin but,' said the girl and Kel hated that because besides the arrogance the kid was right. Nothing was worse than the business of drugs.

She asked what could be done to make her fate better than the one which was destined but the girl said they had no use for her now because they couldn't trust her but Kel knew that already.

'I gave you a chance but there it is,' she continued.

'What you gonna do with Rose?' asked Kel.

'Same as you, swap her for guns.'

'I mean how you gonna treat her.'

'What's it matter to you?'

Kel wanted to say something in her own defence. Anything that would expose the bit of herself that was decent. The part of her that she knew had conscience and empathy wired into its fabric if she only had time and nerve enough to unpick it.

Instead Kel stood at the water's edge and the waves came good and took in most of her legs. She guessed it didn't much matter if they were going to put lead in her back or sink her in the deep, because she was dead anyway.

She turned for one last look at the lighthouse and something about the bright day reflected in one of the windows, finally she knew which room Rose was in, her face pressed against the glass, too late. Kel had been so close, touching distance. She wished there was a way to say truthfully the sorry that was in her and she hoped that Rose knew the remorse she felt inside. Kel wanted to shout it, purge it, prove to Rose that she wasn't a bad person. All the talk of being hard was a lie.

'I do feel things,' she whispered, 'I promise I do.'

'Time to go,' shouted one of the boys when a speedboat circled into view and Kel saw the stolen lifeboat being towed behind it and she wondered at the craziness of the kids. They were going to set her free.

'Time to meet your fate,' laughed the girl. 'Gonna send you packin, leave you way, way out on the ocean without a paddle and see where it gets you. Miserable death I'd say, a miserable death with a million gulls snappin you gone.'

Kel watched her take the oars out of the boat and throw them into the crowd. She climbed into the oarless dinghy and it was too big without Rose and the baby and their faces were everywhere. She sat dumb and pained in its middle and waited to be towed out into the everlasting ocean. Hell on earth heading under.

She was heading the way she'd always known she was heading and when an hour had passed and she was at last cut loose from the speedboat she lay on her back and wondered, as always: why if it was her destiny did it take so long to die?

Kel pulled at what clothes were still holding to hide corners of skin from the bang-bang rain, but no matter what she did the salt-soak still bit biddy bites from her flesh. Death if it was coming for her would arrive at a slip-slow pace and it would pull the sky down on top of her, inch by inch and hour by hour.

The boat had been a cradle for life once and it'd swung in the hope of things, a womb of wonder guiding Kel toward a better fate, but not any more.

The cradle had become a dig-dug grave, a flotsam object heading for the ocean floor and Kel's bones heading the same.

She pushed back to rest her head so she could watch the speedboat retreat and soon nothing but the grey-green wash looked back at her. She wished she had her knife to ease the pain that was loneliness. To cut a line in her arm deep and wide was to let the misery out and what was left of a good world in. She wondered about the green of land and field that was her fantasy of a good life living. In mind her future was painted with a healthy heart and a job that wasn't foot-soldier running and she thought about the drug thing and the shame that lived there and finally above all she thought about Rose and she sat up suddenly.

Kel realised she had never asked Rose about her dreams, never asked her what colours she painted her future. Kel's was green and she smiled a little then because she knew for sure that the girl was all about every shade of pink and maybe that was fine. It was a comfort colour and perhaps the girl needed comfort more than she let on.

Kel wondered about Rose up there in the prison that was the lighthouse and every thought she had in her head had its roots buried in fairytale. Dare and rescue and heroics were all at play inside, and so was something akin to doing the right thing. Rose needed her and Kel liked the idea of that. It was a new thing, but also a good thing.

Kel leaned forward and she bent to reach down into the hallowed depths of water. She cupped her hands as if to swim and turned the water over. If she had no oars she would be her own oar, if she had no map or compass to guide then strength of will would have to do.

Kel knew what way was the right way to head and that was toward the point where she saw the speedboat disappear. So she dipped her head to the waves and closed her eyes and it was as if everything that was inside her was now on the outside, swimming. Swimming to save both the girl and the baby that would in turn save herself.

Chapter Nine

There were times of constant motion when Kel gave herself up to the cause completely, even as the night arrived dark and cold and marked her soul the same. Her eyes were closed to her reflection and her mind was numb to the warm water and cold rain alike and instead she counted round and round until the second night came rolling wrap-around once more.

All she could think about was Rose and then the baby over and over again. Time away from the kid had done something to her whether she wanted it or not. It was as if she had lost some part of her body or a sane way of thinking. Something that needed hauling in was out there and lost in the ether. She could feel it tug at her, a string-thing pulling. It was a ghost feeding, suckling the spirit from her core and replacing it with sandbag guilt. But just as the burden began to feel unbearable, that was when Kel's luck altered its course and the moon poked pretty over the horizon. Its orb was so big and fleshy it filled the dark with muscular bounce and Kel sat up to wash herself clean with midnight light.

And then she saw it, the lighthouse, sitting stupid and struck-down by the beauty of the night. Brought here by fate when she didn't believe in fate, fate and her strength of will.

Kel sat back and let the draw of the tide guide her closer to shore. When the dinghy was close enough to be grounded on the rocks she sat legs dangling in the sea and from there she went fully into the water and swam toward the slipway. She lay on the seaweed slip a moment to catch her breath and watched the lighthouse for shadows and coming-going kids but there were none. No traps, no guards, no nothing: the scene had been set for rescue because it was the right thing to do. Fate and more fate.

Kel lifted herself on to her hands and then her knees and she kept her eyes on the tower. Rose was up there somewhere, up in her tower with the gulls looping low like buzzards closing in for the kill.

She stood with the fight filtering through her veins and growing strong as she prepared herself for the kick and climb. The tide had sucked itself away from the island rock and now nothing but jagged teeth remained. A jaw that threatened to snap tight and keep Kel for the chew. She stubbed her boot tips one-two on to the algae-greased slipway and ran toward the lighthouse like it was a thing for catching.

She was glad to have surprise on her side. The delinquent kids would be spinning drunk someplace dark and damp, she knew this well from her nights kept at the lighthouse. They'd be all settled and unprepared and it meant that if she was careful she might pass them by completely and with that thought she went forward.

'I swear this int what I had planned,' she whispered, her feet slipping on the oily ground. 'It int even near to anythin I thought up.'

She took her time to approach the building and her eyes were peeled to pins for light and shadow and her ears were satellites for listening. Her one chance and the only chance left to get Rose and return her to the beginning of things. Whatever it took she would do it, get things sorted once and for all.

Kel stood against the granite cylinder wall of the light-house and the eternal cold residing there permeated her shirt and stuck to her skin.

She felt her way around each block of stone and her fingers scratched and dug into the crevices as if she were hanging over some deep water ravine, with life and death and everything that was body dangling in the balance. And this was how she worked her way to the door at the front of the lighthouse.

She stood with an ear pressed into the iron and listened out for the sound of banter boys and girls but nothing but the big-bully ocean shouted back. So she held her breath and slowed her heartbeat down to a tick and took a moment to look through the window that was a circle in the door. She heard nothing and she saw nothing, and that could be good or it could be bad. Kel held her chest a moment more before reaching out a hand and putting it to the doorknob and grip-ping it tight. The silence meant one of two things. Either the feral kids with the bad running riot in their veins were wasted, clumped together in a heap somewhere, or they had seen her approach the shore and were lying in wait in the cold-cut shadows.

She turned the screw that held the door shut and pushed forward and stepped into the place that was freedom to the kids and prison to Rose and she did not stop. She went slow past a room with the breath of sleeping children circling and on toward the stairs and she negotiated them in the sticky soot of pitch black night.

She wondered if there was still a way to execute her plan. The thought that she was risking her life for Rose just to have her saved confused Kel. To give the girl back her life because she had been the one to take it, had snatched it from her without asking. Maybe there was something close to remorse residing within Kel, but even still, her actions confused her. Why was she risking her own life just to save Rose from the fate that she herself had planned for the rich tower girl?

She stabbed a toe to each step and bent her knees to take the noise out of her movement and she kept her head up because there would be a guard at Rose's door and a guard meant giveaway light.

It wasn't long before the dark of vertical tunnelling gave way to grey and Kel saw the end to the climb at last. She slowed to a creep and kept her eyes on the circle of light that grew and swung before her and on the hand that held the gas lamp because that was the hand of foe. This was it, this was the moment when her heart must not fail her. The one-stop breath where things would come good. A split-reed second where she would disarm the boy that guarded her and save Rose and the baby and get gone and running without anyone knowing otherwise.

As she crept closer she could see it was the pushover boy and she smiled to herself because she knew this would be easy.

She could see by the half-tipped bottle of contraband settled in his lap and the way his head tilted sideways that this would take no time at all. She stepped into the light with battle on her mind and in her hands and she flexed her fingertips and snapped them ready.

'You,' said the boy and he blinked and rubbed his eyes to see good the thing he was seeing. 'You int sposed to be here.'

Kel shrugged and thought it a funny thing for him to say. She stepped forward and the boy was slow to move, blade blinking and turning over in his hands and Kel could see it was her knife. The one decent possession she had to her name and the only possession just about.

'That's mine,' she said.

'Not any more,' said the boy. He raised it to her face and Kel started to smile. 'What you grinnin at?' He narrowed his eyes.

'You, what's with the attitude?' She stepped forward.

'Stop,' he shouted. 'Stay where you are.'

'Or what?

He flashed the knife and told her she should have listened to him.

'Bout what?'

'About everythin.' He passed the knife from his left hand to his right and Kel nodded and prepared herself for the smash.

'What you noddin at, donkey is you?'

He expected an answer but Kel didn't bother with the kind of talk boys liked, bravado and huff-puff smoke without fire. She swung her left arm into the hand with the sweeping knife and she caught it by the shank and pulled the boy to the ground. When he started to shout she tugged at his hoody and stuck it into his mouth for the shut-up.

She left him tied with his own clothes knotted and his belt she buckled to blood around his mouth to keep his shouting buried deep within his belly.

Silence. Kel closed her eyes and listened out for the kids at the bottom of the lighthouse. Were they waking up? She wasn't sure, a few mumbled words perhaps, were they getting louder? She stood and looked at the two doors that the boy had been guarding and went to them. 'Rose,' she whispered. 'Rose, where the hell are you?' She tried the handle of each door and found them locked.

Behind the fourth door she could hear shouting and it hammered into her when she heard Rose call out her name. Kel knew there were no more than three free minutes available to them. A small window of opportunity in which to crawl before somebody heard the lad's muffled shouts and saw the two girls creeping about their stronghold. With this knowledge she kicked the boy shut to buy them a moment's grace and she bent to pick her knife off the floor and sheathed it and found a key in his jeans pocket and went to the door.

'Rose?' she whispered as she put the key into the lock and twisted.

'What took you so long?' the girl asked.

'Shush, you gotta be quiet.' She opened the door and when the girl hugged her suddenly she pushed back the brief moment of affection, confusing, surprising. 'We got to get goin.' She picked up the baby and when the baby smiled at her she put it quick into Rose's arms and turned and the girl followed.

They took their time to negotiate the thin-tip steps and Kel kept one hand to the curved wall to steady herself and the other she kept gripped tight around her knife. She could hear the heavy in-out of Rose's breathing behind her and the rise and fall of her own and she swallowed hard to get the buzz of concentrated silence out of her ears. They were nearly there. She could see the smear of moonlight as it reflected through the window in the door and could smell the stench of putrid kids pickled in booze and heard their open-mouthed snores and snoring was good. She was going to get away with it, finally things were heading toward right.

When they reached the front door she put a finger to her mouth and felt for the doorknob and turned it slowly.

'Shit,' she whispered, 'somebody's locked it.'

'There's got to be another way out,' said Rose, 'at the back, maybe, come on.' She passed the baby to Kel and they retraced their footsteps back through the lighthouse.

Kel could hear voices, they were definitely louder now, two and then three. She hoped the boy didn't come to, if he did it was game over. She followed Rose further on toward the back of the lighthouse and all the while she could hear more voices behind them.

'No turnin back,' said Kel. 'Em kids are up.'

'There's a window,' whispered Rose, 'and I can see a crack in it.'

They both held their breath as Rose pushed at the glass until it fell on to the ground outside and together they climbed through the gap, passing the baby as they went.

'Go slow,' said Kel, but when the baby started to cry they ran for their lives.

Outside the lighthouse Kel took a minute to take stock of her surroundings. She could see the dinghy was where she had left it, but she needed to find the oars, quickly. She closed her eyes and told herself to believe in fate, it had brought her this far.

'Please,' she shispered, 'I'll never ask for nothin, but I'm askin for this.'

They needed to get away from the lighthouse.

Kel shouted for Rose to get into the dinghy and as she skidded down the slipway she spied a rack stuffed with wood, junk and two day-glo oars poking from underneath, and she was quick to pull them free and run as fast as she could toward the boat and jumped in.

They left the island under a sky full of star-light bullets and nothing but pure stupid luck kept them alive long enough to row toward a slipstream undercurrent pull that dragged them cheering from the lighthouse.

The two girls lay a long time beneath the true-blood stars of forever night, and when Rose asked if she thought the kids might give chase Kel had no puff left in her to answer yes or no or otherwise.

For that one moment they were free of all the wrong things. Maybe now Kel could think about saving herself.

She sat up in the boat and looked at the girl and she looked at her a long time.

'What?' said Rose.

Kel shrugged.

'Are you waiting for me to thank you? Because it's not going to happen.'

Kel smiled and she lay back with the happy of company coursing through her veins. Before that moment she had never known companionship enough to lose it and then to miss it; it was an incredible, unbelievable thing.

'I should be sunning myself on some beach someplace hot, Miami or somewhere,' Rose laughed and she sat forward and looked out at the ocean and then back at Kel. 'Truth is I didnt think I'd see you again. I suppose I'm grateful for that.'

Kel nodded and she lifted the baby from the centre of the boat for the sake of it.

'The big hero come to save the day.'

Kel shook her head and said it wasn't like that and then she wondered what it *was* like. Had she honestly been thinking there was one last chance left at spearing her plan? A last-ditch attempt at stabbing a bullseye out of her future?

She continued to look at the girl and she knew as if she was in any doubt that something else was at play. Kel wished she didn't care about the little-miss rich girl, but the fracture that had happened in her had pulsed with pain, an ache that was all wrong and strange and maybe incredible the same. The feeling was scary new but so great that for a moment she had to put a hand to her heart in the hope that it might steady itself no matter how briefly.

'You OK?' asked Rose.

'Course, why you ask?'

'Your heart.'

Kel nodded. 'I'm just grateful for the calm.' She picked up the baby and turned to feed it.

'Did you miss him?' asked Rose.

'No.'

'Ha, you missed him, big softy.'

Kel ignored her. She was enjoying the peace of nothing doing nothing needing to be done.

'He missed you,' continued Rose.

'That's cus he sees me and sees food.'

'We got any left?' asked Rose.

Kel moved forward and opened the storage pocket where they had stored food.

'Nothin,' she said.

'Not even the rice and pasta?'

Kel gestered to the empty space.

'Well that's a shame, what about the other side?'

'Just my bag, spose they dint find it much use.'

Kel looked over the edge of the boat. 'I could try fishin again.'

'You want to?'

Kel shrugged. 'Maybe later.'

She tightened the baby in its blankets and passed it to Rose. 'You two might just as well sleep for a while.'

'What about you?'

'I int tired. Besides, we might just make land by sun up.'

Kel watched Rose make herself comfy on the floor of the boat with the baby in her arms, he looked perfect there. She told herself a few hours rowing away from the lighthouse and she would soon spot land.

Hours passed, how many Kel didn't know; her mind was taken up by the sky and sea and moon, everything startling and swollen in size. The wind had picked up and with it came bumping clouds the size of mountains.

When the first drops of rain appeared through the gloom all Kel knew of them was the spirals they made out at sea and she watched them dip and pock the water into beautiful spin-top patterns. She took off her jacket and leaned to put it over Rose and the baby and sat back to let the rain soften her shoulders and arms. To feel the thing fully was to know the thing in its entirety, there was a storm out there close and closing and bigger than before and it was heading their way.

'It's raining,' said Rose suddenly.

Kel looked at her and said perhaps the storm wouldn't be as bad as it looked. 'Maybe it'll turn back round. Go back to sleep.'

'I'm awake now.' Rose sat up and pushed into the stern of the boat. 'You see land yet?'

'Can't be far off.' Kel thought of all the ways to take the girl's mind from the storm. Perhaps if she asked about her dreams they would have somewhere to start from, a little hope in which to crawl and hide from the encroaching squall, take their minds off.

'You asked me backalong bout my life,' said Kel, 'but I never asked you bout yours, not properly.'

'So?'

'So you must be missin home, missin things bout home.'

Rose rubbed her eyes and yawned, 'What do you care?' she asked.

'Cus it's my fault, all this is my fault. Like you said.'

'And you want to talk about my life now? Hello!' Rose gestured toward the rain clouds that were closing in all around them.

'That's what we do,' said Kel. 'We talk to take our minds off it.' She sat forward. 'Tell me bout your childhood.'

'You think my life is perfect, don't you?'

'I never said that.'

'Well, I told you, it's boring. Was boring. I ask for whatever I want and get whatever I want.'

'Sounds OK to me.'

'It seems like a lifetime ago now, anyway.'

Kel watched Rose make a fuss of her hair, twist the blonde strands into a knot. She seemed anxious, reality had caught up with her.

'Wish I knew how far out we are,' said Kel.

'I just wanted to know something more than four square walls and the sky,' Rose continued. 'I was sick to the gut of all the pampering and the partying, if I'm honest with you.'

Rose looked at Kel and said people had a mind for thinking life in the towers was paradise and whilst it was close to perfect, perfection wasn't everything.

'Well you got what you wished for, dint you?' said Kel. 'Adventure and all that.'

Rose nodded. 'You know, when we saw all the horror back at Falmouth and the towers without light, I was terrified, but a part of me was excited too, because at least it was different. Now though, after everything, I hope things haven't changed. Not too much anyway. I think maybe it's time to head home.'

'The idea you had to run, you have that a long time?' Kel asked.

Rose nodded.

'You tell anyone?'

Rose shrugged and said she had told her friends.

Some friends, thought Kel, friends that had unwittingly set in motion an uncertain fate for their friend. She supposed it was the same person that had thought up the kidnap idea in the first place and it was all fate related. She wanted to press Rose for more, but when she looked starboard to where the sky was darkest she knew the storm would not be long in falling.

Just a little teacup storm she told herself and then the calm would return.

Kel dipped down into the boat. She told Rose to rest awhile if she could and she too closed her eyes so she might have a moment removed from fear. She thought about her heart fixed up right and went on toward her happy place of good clean country living. She painted it green and blue and framed it plain and she held on to that picture perfect for as long as she could. But soon fantasy fanned itself into tiny feathers of fingering doubt and the worry about this storm transformed into the thought of a storm long past and Kel was back in the cabin in the woods. The time of thinking started as a usual night, window sitting and staring blank when the generator flooded. Silent and watching her reflection in the candlelight, listening to the creek of tree and brush of bow, everything fingers, pushing for the break.

She sat in the bedroom that was everyone's room and told herself that the storm was nothing to get worried about because all the flooding and the smashing of things had happened already. All the trees that could come down had done so and that was good because it meant firewood for the stove and all the broken gates and fences were fine because by morning they would be chained back good as.

Another storm and another night left alone because Kel was the youngest and all the others sixteen and older were out on the drink. Kel didn't mind the loneliness so much back then, and if she had known what was coming she wouldn't have minded the lonely one tiny bit.

Kel supposed she was nearly fourteen in her memory, nearly fourteen and not yet gone to school and not about to go to school. She must have been nearly fourteen because she remembered it as winter and whilst she wasn't good at counting she knew her birthday was in spring and the baby came in the autumn time.

Kel went on digging into her recollections to keep the ocean storm at bay and she tightened her eyes for detail, but that one-time thing that happened had kept on happening a hundred times until her memories of it were just patchwork snatches.

Each time she thought she might make sense of the patching and stitching, her world unravelled all over again. The thing that happened in the lightless storm night and then kept happening and the baby that came because of it was one of those unravelling things.

She opened her eyes to look at the baby burrowed in the centre of the boat and she kept her eyes on it until it moved and then she sighed.

'You were sleeping,' said Rose.

'No I weren't.'

'You had your eyes closed.'

'Had my eyes closed but weren't sleepin.'

'What then?'

'Thinkin.'

'About what?'

'Other storms.'

'Worse than this one?'

'A thousand times worse.'

'I doubt that.'

The boat was moving where it chose now, pitching high on the peaks of waves, and Kel knew that the here and now was about to go one of two ways.

'Might not be so bad,' she said to Rose and when the girl couldn't hear her she shouted it and she leaned forward a little to see if she believed her.

'I doubt that too,' said Rose and Kel shrugged.

'What are we going to do?' asked Rose.

'Wait.'

'And then what?'

'Wait some more.' Kel wanted to tell Rose that things would be all right, same as her two older sisters used to say to her, but just like then she knew things weren't right, so instead of soothing words she stared down the storm because to know your enemy was to have some understanding of the intricacies of fate.

The pattern of weather had turned toward them. It spun the boat and twisted it and hollowed out a well of water for it to drop right into. Down into the depths of the ocean they crashed, all the way down to the sea bed and up to the clouds and back they bounced like sinking, throwing stones.

'Hold on,' Kel shouted to Rose and she jammed herself into the belly of the silly rubber boat. Nothing but thin rip material sat between them and the deep and Kel knew it was only a matter of time before the towering waves climbed so high there would be no space left in the clouds for building and they would tumble down around them.

'We've had it,' shouted Rose and she clambered toward Kel in an attempt to talk.

'Stay put,' shouted Kel above the roar. 'Stay put and wrap the baby to your back or else you'll have us tipped completely.'

'We've got to bail out the boat,' Rose shouted. 'Look.' She shifted her weight so Kel could see the puddle of water she was sitting in and they worked with the oars to splash what they could from the dinghy. Nothing else mattered in that last moment but the rallying for survival. Kel knew she had it in her to keep digging the water from the boat longer than all the puff the storm had in it.

There were times when the rain fell lightly and played out on the wind and Kel was sure the waves had lessened slightly and this was when they stopped to catch their breath. They sat with the lamp relit and glowing dumb-dull between them and watched the scrawling morning clouds circle the horizon like a pack of wild things stalking their prey.

'Do you think the storm's coming back?' asked Rose.

'I know it,' said Kel and she nodded toward the splinters of light that cracked the dawn into two parts, night and day.

'I guess there's no point paddling.'

'Paddlin where?'

'Away from the storm.'

Kel shook her head, she knew it would get them no matter what. She wished there were words that could be said to ease Rose's worry. Something with the 'all all right' stuffed into it. She opened her mouth but all that sounded was her clicking, tutting tongue.

They sat like good-kid schoolkids and looked out at the mute morning that flashed black and then white. The storm was something for staring at and something for staring down. Maybe if they didn't blink the storm would blink first and implode suddenly a good distance from the boat, spiral into the sea and go cold, become a drop in the ocean like a dead thing nothing thing.

Kel couldn't take the chance and she took her bag from the place she had hidden and secured it days earlier and she put her notebook and the things not lost in the bounce into the plastic sack that once stored food and tied it tight and knotted to her belt. A last-ditch attempt at survival because survival was in her. Nothing else remained but to do the thing that might save her, the thing that had saved her her whole life over, to be calm because calm kept some kind of head upon her shoulders.

She gave Rose the spare carrier bag and told her to fill it with air and to hang on to the rope that threaded its way around the edge of the dinghy and she did the same till her wrists were bound blue and cutting. To hold on to the boat was to have the boat because without it there would be no second chance. Kel looked across at Rose and she could see

163

panic pooled in her eyes and she told her to zip the baby into her mac and not to think of anything past the here and now. She shouted hard above the deafening din and her mouth ripped wide with salt-water filling and she coughed and spat it back in defiance.

The boat pitched and rolled as the wind and waves bloated and coiled and crashed around them. A monster thing and a devil thing soaring high above as they ploughed into the green water darkening, pulling them under.

Beneath the waves the storm was nothing but silence. Silence and movement. Everything that was out was in and everything that was in was out. They were a part of and apart from the gale force skin-strip winds that finally hooked the boat and flipped it, silent dark and wondering.

Deep dark down they remained for the longest time at the bottom, top, middle of the nowhere ocean. It was and then it wasn't all the same. Another world entirely that Kel had no option but to let in; the salt leeched into her veins and the weeds stuck to skin and everything was filling and strangling, pulling her down further into the chasm and weighting her gut with sand and grit and stone.

Kel let her limbs fall free of fighting and she gave herself up fully to the float. There was no point battling the inevitable. She would succumb to the fate the stars had inked out for her before birth and leave nothing but the remaining space.

Kel Crow would either die or she would live. To know that the end was close was to be at peace with that knowledge and she let the warm salt water sting her flesh and shrink her down to the size of what remained of her heart, a floating bag of not much at all. Perhaps in death she could work at the penance set for the crimes she had committed, exorcise the badness from her. Then maybe the forgiveness she yearned for would finally come good. At times Kel sat bobbing in the soapy sup and she wondered if death was merely the same rewind over and over. Silently waiting and then silently waiting all over again, with no beginning to mark and no end in sight. What did it matter if she lived or died? Nobody would miss her, she had no one in her life except the baby.

'Rose,' she whispered. She lifted her head high above the water and said the girl's name again and then she shouted it, 'Rose, Rose, Rose.' She looked across the rolling waves and wished she could see what it was that was beauty about the girl. Sometimes she swam but mostly she merely hung like a peg-line rag and watched the rain ping about her and tasted the drops as they clung to her face. She untied the bag from her belt to hold. The air that she had made sure to trap there kept her afloat.

There were times when she thought she heard Rose call out her name and she shouted that she was *here here here* but then nothing. The girl was gone and not just gone but struck absolutely from the earth complete. When the time came for the storm to dig its claws in someplace else, Kel had settled into a belly bubble of sleep. Exhaustion had her and it had her completely. Mostly drifting was better than mostly sinking and she kept her fingers twisted to the plastic wrap and rested her head sideways to the cushion. The warm waves carried Kel from where the boat had capsized and slowly she closed her eyes to the black and blue of them. Pain and fear combined gave way to letting go and when the last of the buoyancy in her belly bubbled from her lips she felt herself drop like a stone. If this was it then this was it. Death in the dark relentless depths of a billion acres of ocean; a gut full of empty and then a gut full to heaving with seawater splutter and it was all the same. The wet rot would get her after all and she would turn inside out and slack-skinned and Kel Crow would be no more.

There was something about setting her name loose that made her think about her bastard kin, and then she thought about the baby Crow and she wondered what name might go on its gravestone if it had one, and if not a stone then perhaps a cross of wood meant for kindling. It was then that a tiny light sparked up in her and it gave her such a jolt to think the fight thing was still in her that she kicked her feet and fired her arms pointing up back towards the surface. One more breath to stay alive and then another to have her work stuff through. Her life was not over, would not be until she said so. She drifted wherever the waves dictated, occasionally catching the air in a vice like gristle between her teeth and she chewed it over and in and made the most of breathing before being pulled under once again. Minutes felt like hours and hours like days. Her bundle of things was buoyant in her arms like the baby she had lost and she talked to it as if it were so. They were in this together and they would live it and fight it and they would survive it together too.

Soon a little morning light soothed the sea and Kel took comfort in its lullaby rocking. Anything that took her mind off the shrivelling wet was worth something and she hummed some kiddie tune that was all songs of childhood combined. Songs that she had heard sung and had memorised through the spying and listening at the windows and doors of good god-fearing folk.

When morning arrived properly Kel greeted it with relief. A bit of storm light was better than no light and it returned the grown-up to where the child had begun to show. She told the sack not to expect any kind of conversation today because it was just a sack and she used the brief moment of clarity to look for wounds. She felt for the cut on her head and the big plump-berry lump that it had become. She looked over her hands in turn and everything was shedding and falling away. The rot had settled in as she knew it would; the skin dividing into scaling flakes and the nails raised and stirring in their beds. If rescue did not happen today she doubted she would get through another night.

When the wind picked up, Kel knew for certain that she would not.

For a girl who liked to plan, waiting on nothing much more than the sureness of death was hard. Without control she was driftwood, something bitten and rubbed out fully until nothing remained but water. She might as well be back at the shack, beat and tied and too tired to fight when Dad came drunk and sniffing.

She closed her eyes because they burnt with the effort of staring down the waves and she settled her head into the bin-bag bubble and it was a pillow on a bed in a house that she would never know.

Kel spotted some of their things strewn about the beach and told herself she should collect them because there was nothing else to the place besides sand and rock and the damn ocean surround. She wondered if anybody was about. What part of Cornwall was this?

She walked the cove a little and when she stood to face the cliff she eyed it for possible climbing splits in the rock but there were none. Nothing but slippery block levels of pink and grey slate and the fall-away scree that pooled in the ridges.

For the billionth time in her life Kel Crow was alone. More than that; it was as if she were the last person standing. She was just a dead-beat girl alone on the planet, not the battle-hungry battle-scarred warrior she thought. She was tired and hungry and worn through to her weak strangling bones. She kicked about in the sand and flicked it at the cliffs and she bent to pick up the oddments of torn clothes and busted nothings and brought them together in a bundle, the only things to bring colour to the slate-grey landscape.

Kel piled the detritus into the opening of a scoop-out cave that she thought would make a great shelter later and then she entered the low-ceiling cavity for the water she might find there and she was right. Fresh water funnelled in a life-line drip from a fissure deep within the rock and she lay on her back to let it fill her mouth and she swallowed it down as if it were the last thing on earth worth knowing because it was. It tasted of summer dew and summer rain combined. Kel thought of the fields and plants that might have captured that rain above the mountainous cliffs and the thought of dry land had her smile a little. Maybe this really was the mainland, perhaps at any moment somebody would call down to her from the clifftop, throw down a rope and tell her to hurry up and climb, that they had a fire going, food cooking. She was alive and maybe Rose and the baby were alive the same. It had only been a few hours since the boat capsized. Perhaps they had already been rescued and were warming themselves by the fire, waiting for Kel.

She drank until her stomach clenched with hunger and then she rolled free of the spring and crawled from the cave and looked toward the cliff, nobody yet.

'Food,' she said.

Kel returned to the shoreline to find something to chew on, picked a fistful of fingering bladderwrack seaweed from the beach and flicked it free of grain and she thought of all the ways to eat the stuff other than ripping and chewing but in the end that was just what she did. It wasn't much, but a country girl like Kel knew that somewhere in that plant lived life. Life enough to have her climb the cliff that would bring her to the clifftop and perhaps lead her to Rose. Kel knew the girl was alive though all her unconscious senses said otherwise, she told herself Rose was breathing still because she had to be. The girl was hers for caring and more than that she was hers for saving.

She settled back down into the damp sponge grit with the taste of salt in her mouth and everywhere else besides and pushed her toes deep into the sand. Her boots were long gone and her one good pair of socks gone the same. They were out there floating somewhere. Maybe the tide would wash them close, but more than likely they were gone forever. They were great boots and Kel felt sorry for their passing, a million miles of walking had been trodden into the story of those boots. A few good runnings had been stamped there too.

She watched the sun hang in the balance between two banks of cloud and as its thin-reed light fired down on to the beach bay its reflection sparked from the sudden revelation rocks. The light put movement into everything solid and when Kel leaned back to stop the spin, she wondered if she had hit her head on the rocks as she was swept ashore. She felt her head for new bumps and closed her eyes to stop the giddy, but when she opened them the rock in front of her that had moved most was moving still.

Another chance offering itself up as good fortune, Kel thought, and she jumped to her feet and she ran to the rocks with the girl's name pinned to her lips. But it only took one bad-beat moment more to see her hope dashed against them.

She stood at the edge of the rocks and stared at the dolphin that balanced there. She supposed it was better to be looking at a half-living animal than a half-dead girl and she climbed out on to the rocks to see if there was any way to save it.

Kel squatted beside the creature and when she cupped what little water was contained in the rock pool to wet its back she could see the red in the water darkening to black. What it was to be a stranded animal in the middle of the relentless ocean, stranded and injured and afraid. Kel knew what it was to be all those things, and when she took her knife from her belt and bent to the beautiful beast she recognised everything in its eyes because it was all in hers too; it was fear and it was fear of the known. What had been and what was to come were both the same.

The part of Kel that was human was sorry to do the thing she was compelled to do now, but to know suffering and to witness the slow-peel burn of death for the sake of clean hands was not in Kel's character, and so with all her strength she buried the knife into the strange satin flesh and she made the job quick.

She sat with the dead animal a long time and something of its selfless spirit entered her. Its existence out there on the rocks was company of a kind. She was not alone; animal dead or alive, she was not alone.

Kel looked up at the cliffs and the thought of Rose out there somewhere set a small spur fire beneath her and she washed the blood from her hands and climbed from the rocks and went off back toward the cliff.

She stood at the foot of the precipice and toed the purple slate shingle that had fallen on to the beach in drifts like heavy snow. She walked it back and she walked it forward. No matter how she went about it she would have to scramble on the giveaway surface: and that meant hands and knees all in for the climb of her life. She knew if she could get past the slip and fall she would be able to use her strength to power up the rock face and she told herself it was a cliff just like any cliff she used to climb as a kid. The secret was to keep going, dig bare toes into every crevice and fingertips into each ridge for clinging no matter how narrow the hold.

To keep moving was to be winning in the fight for height and Kel would keep going until the strange new world below made sense to her. To sit at the summit of her surroundings would be to map them and conquer them in some way. So she took a deep breath and shifted forward and made a start at grappling the cutting oddment stones.

There were parts to her that ached a little and other parts that gave way completely and those were the times when she fell flat and sliding into the smack bang and she let the earth move beneath her because what else was there? Occasionally Kel let the ice-marbled shards press too close into her check and in those moments there was something of both life and death within her. The pain sharpened her senses and comforted the same and if it wasn't for the girl in her care and perhaps the baby she really would have given up on the whole survival thing. Maybe there was no point to living for living's sake, Kel didn't know, but there was so much hope in her gut wishing on a better day that there was no argument to it.

No matter how high the cliff face and how long it took to climb, she would stretch out her hands for a firm finger-hold and hitch her toes the same until she found Rose, and the thought of the girl all pink and scrambled in the wash spurred her on.

* * *

Halfway up the cliff all angles changed and Kel took a minute to prepare for the vertical climb. She rested against the cold smooth rock and skimmed her fingertips all ways to get the measure of it and found it was a beast with all the scratches and scars of deceit cut into it.

She thought out every way to conquer the thing but a brain drained of water and nutrients was a dust-bowl full of dry dirt whistling.

'Nothin to it,' she said. 'Nothin but a slow climb, just got to keep my eyes up.'

She could hear the waves taunt her from below, their slow turn up and down the shingle-sand beach a nauseating rhythm that tipped her sideways until all sound clogged together into a deep, fat buzz. But each step she took was a toe-touch toward land; each bloody-fingered rock a claw pulling her up so she could stand astride this world she did not know or understand.

The cliff was a labyrinth of twisted granite shards and slides: similar in its many shades of purple and grey to the Cornish coast, and in its detail too, but everything blown outward and up towards the clouds. The off-cuts and the waste of granite stacks thrown here either for future keeping or to forget. A mountain just about climbing out of the Atlantic like a defiant, neglected piece of moorland jigsaw. Left to its own devices it had grown fierce and proud, all that crazy beauty gone mad.

Still Kel kept on, with her body slapped up against the

stoic rock and everything that was in her gripped tight with concentrated fear. Without fear she would be a twisted corpse ripped on the rocks below, a bloated belly full of the spiteful rising tide.

She leaned into the narrow ledges to rest and shake the life back into her numb hands and flick the blood from the fingers and she wondered about mortality and kept from looking anywhere but up and out at the constant bastard sea. But still the grey, tedious ocean stretched and gummed its way into the corners of her eyes and it adhered to the sky and pulled it crashing toward her. The magnitude of it haunted Kel and it would haunt her for a long time to come. She watched as the strange daylight pulled clouds from all four corners of the earth. Their shadows crept about the cliff face like things undead. Spirits of stranded wreckers and starved bootleggers and the mere unlucky slunk sideways and up-ways and all ways toward Kel and still she went on to get the better of the madness that was this place. The thought of never seeing the girl again and that of the baby was everything to her and it was this that had her turn back into the rock with the final push upon her. She would get to the top no matter what.

An hour dragged by and in time a good wind came to tie and knot her to the cliff face. It was cold, but cold was good because it kept Kel from thirst and slapped her alert, and when she reached the summit she stretched out her hands to catch the cool racing wind and she held it to her until the ache fell from her bones and the boil simmered from her blood.

Kel sat down and she sat for a good while. There was nothing left in her. The sumit was nothing but a small plateau of rock with the strange plants twisting across it. Where were the fields? Where were the crops that she imagined grew up here? She watched a flock of seagulls navigate the landscape. Sometimes they landed to eye the amusement that was Kel, muttering and mingling amongst themselves, and Kel asked them if they had seen Rose and they had not. But still she called out the girl's name and turned an ear out of the wind in the hope that she might hear her call back.

She stubbed her heels into the sop earth and kicked double to prove that she was still alive and stood up. The realisation that she was not on the mainland dawned upon Kel slowly.

'This is not Cornwall,' she said. 'This is an island.' She put her hand to her chest and closed her eyes, felt the sting of tears as they pushed into her eyes.

'No,' she said, 'no, no, no!' She shouted until the seagulls took flight and her ears pulsed with pain and she screamed until finally her voice snapped, went silent.

She opened her eyes and looked at her feet with the blood on blood and at the roping plants that snaked and bundled crazy about her ankles and wiping her face with her T-shirt she told herself to get a grip, hold on, work out a track for herself that would lead down to the other side of the island. This was all she could do, all she needed to do. It was good to be walking, it meant she was doing something other than thinking. It was strange to be stepping on to unyielding earth after so many days at sea. Her legs wandered everywhere except where she was heading and she cursed them and slapped them straight. She was grateful for the downhill incline because there was not one bit of puff left in her.

Within five minutes by Kel's reckoning she had reached the other side of the island summit. She stood at the stub-end of the rock and bush and peered down into the void below. Here everything was washed with a clearer brush and to her relief everything was closer. The strange island had redeemed itself slightly; it was the shape of a rearing shark, and here Kel stood on the slope of its neck having scaled its snaggle teeth and snap-trap jaws. The thing really was a monster and Kel had the dumb sucker scaled and conquered and wrestled into submission. Below her was a beach, a hundred metres ahead at most and every bit of it a stroll.

Kel stepped off the bony headland and down the earthy banks of the west-facing bay and she had energy enough to curse the ocean tides for stranding her on the other side of the island and she called out to Rose as she scanned the beach. Here and there the storms had washed up a little more of what Kel recognised as theirs and it made her sick with worry, but she told herself to take comfort in the knowledge that they were here somewhere.

She saw her shirt lapping with the tide and she picked it up and hugged it, tied it about her waist and continued with her search.

Daylight was slipping from the sky and with it the tide that had been pulled from the beach and it was replaced with slipping rocks. Kel was careful not to cut her feet further as she stepped through the rock pools and all the while she called out for the girl that was in her care. If she could find Rose then perhaps she would find something inside herself worthy of existence, a tiny piece of compassion that beat within and that she never knew she possessed until now.

At last her feet found rock pressed smooth and flat, and the tiny moment of comfort had her sit and she put her hand to her chest suddenly to feel her heart beating strange as usual and she took comfort in that. To have it beat at all was something, she told herself, and then she said it out loud like a mantra because out there on that island there was not one other bit of good or happy or hope.

She thought about what fate had dealt her and couldn't make sense of it. Even a girl like her didn't deserve this.

She put her knees to her chest and rested her head and arms wherever and she bit back the need to cry and she thought about the cabin in the woods to put the toughness back in. The place that was home but wasn't, the point of escape that she would never rid from her thoughts, from her flesh, whilst the baby lived.

'The baby,' she said, and she opened her eyes and said it again, and for the first time she kept from thinking about the part of the child that was half bad and her mind settled instead on the part that was good, the part that was her.

'My baby,' she shouted and she stood with the panic of parenthood in her and she shouted until her throat choked dry.

She stood to chart the sea as far as it bothered to stretch and then she stopped to look back at the island, and that was when she saw the familiar flash of orange that was the boat and the drift of limbs come unstuck in the shallows that sluiced the foot of the beast.

Each step Kel took towards the boat was a slip-cut fall and it took every scrap of stamina she had not to buckle completely. Occasionally she looked down at her feet and she noticed blood and the trail of footprints they left behind. Proof that she had come and proof that she had gone, herself a ghost passing through, the same as all the other stepping-stone spirits that surrounded her. She felt their meanness streaking on the wind as they tried to push her to her knees and saw their roaming shadows gather up above her on the ridgeline from where she'd come. They shouted profanities and chanted that the girl and the baby were dead dead dead.

Maybe they were, Kel thought. But maybe there was still something of light-life catching in them, a slow-beat heart that drummed low to the ground.

'Rose.' Kel said the name over to keep the girl with her and she felt her neck for pulse and when the baby that was wrapped in the deflated boat stretched up to her she cuddled him so close she thought she might never let go.

'Rose,' she shouted, 'I know you int dead, you gotta wake up.' Kel shook her and then she noticed the leg that was hitched-up wrong and twisted in the rock pool.

The girl had suffered enough. She shouted this to the taunting sea and the chanting island spirits that had come to watch the show; the story of a dead girl and a starving baby and a girl with madness threading like crazy-wire through her veins.

Kel didn't know what was real and what was muddle-minded but as she looked down at Rose's leg she saw the white tooth bone stick clean from the distended flesh. She had seen worse in her life of redneck rioting, she had seen broken bones split the sinews of both the living and the dead. But for a girl who was usually all pretty and precise it rubbed all wrong and Kel knew she would have hated that. The thought started as a tickle in the back of her throat and it made her smile despite tears of despair.

A good mind told her not to touch the wound, but curiosity for what it was that made up animal was in her and the hand not holding the baby went close to it and settled in the blood slop puddle where they both sat.

Kel must have sat there in the leaving rock-pool tide for the longest time, because when Rose asked her what she was doing she could barely see the girl for the dim drag of darkness that had descended upon them.

'Rose?' Kel leaned forward to find the light that made the girl complete.

'Kel? Are we all right?'

Kel nodded and said that they were all alive and breathing and that was one thing and then she looked off toward the cliffs to check for the goading shadows and was relieved to see they had gone.

'What happened?'

'We capsized,' Kel said.

'I kept trying to stay awake, but my leg hurts so badly.' The girl went to sit up and Kel told her not to.

'It hurts like hell, is it OK?'

Kel didn't know what to say but Rose sensed something wasn't right.

'What?' she asked.

Kel shook her head and told her not to move.

'Is it broken? Tell me, please.' She tried to twist to see it.

'Dunno, maybe.' Kel put the baby down so she could hold Rose's head and told her not to move until she knew what was what.

Rose sighed and Kel could see tears building in her eyes.

'Kel. How much worse can it be?'

'You could have cut an artery.'

'With what?'

'Broken bone.'

'Oh God, I'm going to die, and not just die but slowly bleed to death.'

Kel told her to stay still.

'This is all your fault.' Rose moved her head away from Kel. 'I hate you.' She lay dumbstruck with fear. Kel let the horror of living sit between them.

She told Rose that there was no way that with her leg as it was she could make it over the summit of the island and back down the side of the cliff. She told her they would have to wait for the tide to come back in instead, so she could swim her off the rocks toward the shore.

'Why?' asked Rose.

'Why what?'

'Why move?'

'There's caves on the other side of the island. Shelter. There's no shelter on this side and we need shelter to survive.'

'We need a lot of things.'

Kel ignored her and said for now they needed to get her on to the beach this side and out of the wet and see what they could do for her leg at least and they waited until the tide was right.

When the moment finally arrived it was loaded with the weight of killed time and the screaming, spiralling girl had nothing but loathing splitting her lips. Kel tried soft-soap talk and grown-up shouting, but nothing came out right and soon she settled herself into the calm indifference that she was known for.

She waited for the surrounding rock pools to fill and make islands of the highest rocks and when a path big enough for easy passage was set between them and the shore she pulled the orange rubber sheet from the nipping barnacle ridge and floated Rose and the baby back toward the beach. She lay them in the foamy bubbles and told them to not go anywhere whilst she went to find a splint and then she stayed close by for a moment, to see if humour might flick-start the spark back into the girl's eyes, but no. Nothing, just dull-ache marbles staring ahead.

Kel walked the beach and through the dire damp dusk she found a length of wood good enough for setting a leg and she took it back to the girl and positioned it beneath her in the hollow sand. She tied it fast with strips of plastic she'd cut from the boat with her knife.

'I'm gonna pull you up the sand,' said Kel and she told her it would hurt but this was the only option other than drowning and she lay the baby on Rose's chest and set about dragging them a small way from the shore.

'What now?' whispered Rose when they were safe from water.

'We prepare ourselves.'

'What for?'

Kel thought for a minute. 'For being rescued.'

'And when will that be?'

'Any day.' Kel had no way of knowing where they were or if they would be rescued, but she knew she needed to reassure Rose, she had to give her something to hold on to. 'I reckon ships pass by here all the time.'

Kel took what was left of the dead deflated boat into her lap and cut herself two squares of rubber and carried them to the cliff edge and she walked it close, listened for drips falling from the slate above and dug cradles in the sand. Settled the rubber into them to make soft cups.

When they were full enough she took them back and they drank and refilled and drank again and Kel gathered driftwood where she found it in the dark by the touch of foot. What thin drift splints she found she circled and lit with the lighter that was still in her pocket and to her amazement still worked and with tiny light she found better wood and in time they had a fire that gave heat enough for drying. She slashed the last flap of boat and made head and leg bundles for Rose and some kind of pillow bed for the baby. They sat with the dense night weighing down on them and Kel wondered about the dark shadow creatures that patrolled the island. Circling and closing around them like a run of rope ready to lash.

She sat close to the fire and fed it with the damp brittle bone sticks long into the night. She draped seaweed fresh from the surf on to a boulder close to the flames and she turned it and mashed it through and this was what they had to eat. The taste of salt was better than no taste at all and Kel knew from a lifetime of knowing things that there were nutrients in the awkward plant blubber. Nutrients that would keep them alive long enough to figure out what was needed. Kel sat back on her elbows and she chewed the weed down to pulp and then she swallowed hard and waited for the pain in her chest to subside and the dry squeeze of hunger became less so.

She looked up into the sky and followed the arch of its dome from left to right with the baby lethargic but partway feeding from her. Through the thin-skin covering Kel noticed stars wrestling to be seen and she gave them their proper names as always, because those stars were angels and their comfort was everything familiar. She named them as Ursa Minor and Ursa Major and she nodded toward the North Star, Polaris. She had spent most of her short life taking refuge beneath those stars wishing on a better day. Naming them put them at the centre of her universe and she at the centre of theirs. No matter where her day and life ended they were there at the start and would be there at the end and there was comfort in that.

With the passing of the fog came a new kind of night-light to the island and it was as if a lid had been raised and so Kel told her sleeping companions that she was going for a walk. She paced the tideline and watched it deliver fresh seaweed to the shore and what driftwood bobbed there in the wet she lifted up the beach to dry. Water and fire was all they needed for now, and then tomorrow she would float Rose and the baby round about to the better side of the island and together they would plot things and hatch things until just about everything was taken in and accounted for. Kel would build more of a shelter in the cave for when the inevitable storms returned and she would make a spear and stand strong in the current and stab them a big ugly crab. She'd done it a hundred times as a kid with swamp fish. She would pick every last winkle from the rocks for snacks and the rock-pool blennies she'd cook pink to prawns and chew them all day through. They would eat like kings and they would eat like paupers and they would survive as long as it took to survive, as long as it took to be rescued.

Kel walked the length of the beach and she stood at the cut of cliff that wedged itself into the sea and she wondered about that other side of the island and she wondered about it a long time. The odd-job things that had washed up on to shore with her were on that other side too. The useless, broken, bit and bob things that would be useful to them now more than ever; rubbish things and good things the same and from which she could make a world worthy of existence, if only for a day or two. A place to think, a place to replan and work out a way to get off the island.

Out toward the horizon Kel liked to think there was a little shard-light coming. It was not so far since summer after all and the nights were short, even on the daggered dead-end island with its bandit spirits waiting for them to become corpses upon which to feed. Morning would come. It would be a day with all the everyday running through it, Kel would make sure of that.

She stamped her feet one two in the sud-surf and she told herself that she could overcome this land and then she shouted it so that she might hear it fully. There was more world out there than her world and it was no better or worse, but it had the potential for change. Kel could feel her nails hooking a little under the skin of something new: if she could just claw at the flesh that was this new place and pull the skin clean from it she would find something that resembled civilised living, Reveal the bare-bone clues to what it was to live a good life. She would have something to build on, a new world to create.

Kel stood in the water and she watched it climb the cuffs of her jeans and she watched it return to the fiddle and forage of the rock pools. She stood still until her mind was set: if she got off the island alive she would be a better person, and not just a better person but the *best* kind of person. Good heart broken heart she would do it.

Chapter Eleven

At first light Kel found herself lying half-in half-out of the seaweed surf. Exhaustion had taken over and it had taken everything from her in the process.

She wondered how long she had been asleep and tried to make sense of the sky but the white bright clouds were nothing more to her than a headache.

She pulled herself to sitting and looked around at the beach. She shielded her eyes from the dazzling bright of day until she saw Rose and she shouted out her name and went to her.

'You OK?' Kel asked as she crouched in the sand.

'I've felt better.'

'You thirsty?'

Rose nodded and Kel went to fill the water cups. The girl was holding on and that was good. She filled one cup and drank it down and filled it again and carried both to Rose, and together they drank the rubber-band water down into their empty stomachs and then Kel fed the baby with what drop of milk remained in her.

'How is he?' asked Rose.

'Don't think he knows nothin of nothin.'

'That's good.'

Kel looked at her and nodded. She had been wondering about the overturned boat. How Rose had managed to keep the baby afloat, alive.

'What?' asked Rose. 'Why are you looking at me like that?'

'Bout the baby.'

'What about him?'

'How did you keep him alive?'

Rose shrugged. 'I filled that carrier you gave me with air and tied it to his wrist and then we still had the boat. It was a bit deflated but OK for a while.'

'You make it sound easy.'

'It wasn't too bad, not until we hit the rocks anyway. It took everything to keep him from smashing into them.'

'Thank you,' said Kel. 'Thank you for savin him.'

Rose smiled. 'I'd say it was nothing, but ...' She looked down at her leg.

'Thank you,' said Kel again. The words felt strange on her lips; she didn't think she had ever said them and meant them before.

'How is it?' She bent to look at Rose's leg.

'Hurts like hell. How does it look?'

'Bone snapped clean, spose you're lucky.'

'Really? How do you know?'

'It int fractured all ways, clean break right through.'

'And that's lucky?'

'Good you int got no splinters or whatever.'

'And what would happen if I did? Really.'

'You'd bleed to death.'

Kel gave Rose the baby to take her mind off her leg and she sat back on her haunches and told the girl she didn't look so bad considering.

'Well that's good. I'm glad I'm not too sore on the eyes.' Rose looked at Kel and tried to smile. Then she asked what Kel had planned because she could see plotting in her eyes and she had become accustomed to that look.

'We gotta get to the other side of the island.'

'I'm not going anywhere.'

Kel sighed and told her there were things worth having that had washed up on the beach. And there were caves for sleeping in.

'What's wrong with sleeping on the beach?'

'Int goin to stay dry forever. Would be good to have somewhere we can light a fire and stay dry.'

'So what do I have to do?' asked Rose.

'Get your good leg on to what's left of the boat and I'll lift the other.'

'Then what?'

'I'll slide you to the water and then float you round.'

'What about the baby?'

'The same.'

'I don't like this.'

'I don't either, but we're runnin out of options int we.'

The two girls looked at each other and they waited for alternatives to suggest themselves but none did.

Morning came and went with the near corpse dragging and the shouting and screaming along the beach, and when Kel got Rose into the sea she sailed them calmly without word whilst the girl clawed fists of hair from Kel's head. Kel told her this was their only chance at a smooth ride whilst the tide was right and she promised her it would be the last time that she would have to be moved until they were rescued. Kel didn't know if Rose believed her or not and she didn't know if she believed herself, but she pushed on through the water with her feet barely touching base and kept her eyes from looking anywhere but at the rocks that hammered and kicked towards them. To lose sight of direction would be to allow the under-water current to drag them toward the rocky cut and thrust.

The bright-brilliance in the sky outsized all else and it poured light into the ocean like mercury. The silver beads clung to them and curdled the water into an incredible silver embroidered mantle. Everything around them tried to dazzle their eyes shut, but Kel forced hers open in order to guide Rose to safety. Eventually the seawater slipped beneath her waist, and then her hips, and she changed position to pull Rose on to the beach.

They lay side by side on the warm sand with their heads tipped toward where the sun almost split the clouds. The most normal of days laid out Sunday-skimming on the beach, and the strangest one the same.

Kel held her breath and closed her eyes to the tempting warmth and she thought back to the memory of happier times but there were none. Her life was chalked out as a long line of miserable winters, and even the summers consisted of cold wall staring despite the wet and warm. She waited for the inevitable cloud to curtain the sun and when it did she opened her eyes and she looked across at Rose and sighed.

'You ready?' she asked.

Rose nodded. 'It looks like rain might be heading our way,' she said and Kel agreed. A dark thick smudge had come and lodged itself crossways in the sky.

'You ready?' Kel asked again and she bent to the girl and wound the rubber tight in both hands steady for pulling and as Rose shouted and screamed her way up the beach Kel told her she would soon have them a fire lit and hollering up a storm.

She left Rose crying in the entrance of the biggest cave with the baby crying out the same and went to collect the wet and dry and wet again bones of trees. Each twist of weathered wood she dragged toward the cave and the smallest finger-bones she gathered into her shirt tail and these she used as kindling. Everything on the beach had the potential for fire: Kel even picked the scramble knots of rope from the seaweed tideline and smiled at the clots of tar that stuck there.

When everything was piled ready and the fire-pit had been dug and circled with smooth-back stones Kel took her lighter from her pocket and she hit it against her leg and squeezed the wick dry and flicked it into life. She sat with the world heavy on her shoulders and bent to set the tiny flame into the tar-soaked rope and when the flame steadied she cupped it with her hands and fed life into it with the sticks from another land – the bones that had grown and broken and splintered from the earth and had settled on the island for their use only. A gift from the far-end reaches of the planet, Kel supposed.

When the fire came good she looked up to see a fine-comb mizzle had come in from the sea and descended on the island and the way it crawled about the beach had melancholy needled clean through it. She was glad of the heat and light from the fire and was glad of its company as it hid out in the caves with them. The two girls who were neither strangers nor friends stared into the new place of colour. The warmth that circled the low cubby rock behind them hugged their shoulders close and it snuggled the baby the same.

'Could almost be cosy,' said Kel. 'Almost.' As she peered around she saw the firelight continue on, beyond the cave wall.

'What are you looking at?' asked Rose.

'Back there, through the crack, looks like this cave leads somewhere.'

'Don't tell me, more caves.'

'You reckon?' Kel pressed herself up against the wall of the cave and felt the contentment that had engulfed her seep away.

'Who cares,' said Rose.

Kel sighed. She sat forward to look past the flames at the slap-back rain that now thundered from the sky. 'I should look for food.'

'I can wait for food if you can,' said Rose. 'Now you're halfway to getting dry you might just as well dry out completely.'

Kel shrugged. She wanted to have something in her stomach besides water, but the warmth was heaven and it was pulling her toward sleep.

'Maybe I'll wait out the rain,' she said and she reached for a great hulk of wood to haul on to the fire. She held her hands to the heat until the palms pricked with pain and then she lay down.

Kel told herself that she needed to make a new plan. A plan that had a start and an end with all the steps that meant survival stuffed between. She had found shelter, soon she would find food. She looked deep into the flames. 'Tomorrow I'm goin to make a rescue fire,' she said and she promised herself this.

She made the best of turning into the womb of the cave and Rose did her best of doing the same with the baby bundled to her.

She'd take a couple hours' sleep and a couple hours' heat to have her come good before night fell proper, or so Kel thought. She had not reckoned on tiredness so weighted that the night fell with a grave thump and it stuffed the castaways deeper into the cave and down into the heart of the island, where sleep and hunger and exhaustion was a thing akin to dying.

Kel fell to sleep and she fell to dream, and in the dream the sun shone at a constant and was smiling warm. It followed her as she went about her this and that chores and stood at her side as she climbed the hill that was her fantasy hill with the little new shack house on top that was her house. A house with a fence and a gate where she could sit and swing out above a land good and even and dry enough for tilling.

In the dream that was her go-to dream she saw rivers run in silent spirit form and the distant sea kept mindful of the cliffs to expose settling sand on each and every coast. Everything opposite to the way things were. No place sodden and rotting and no social boundaries in any case. All citizens equal in a new world cared for long enough to have the balance brought back into play.

When finally Kel awoke several hours had passed. She lay in the slot between reality and fantasy and watched the perfect orbs of subterranean water bloat and fall from the cave walls all around them. She stretched out a hand to catch a little of the sup and when Rose woke she did the same.

'Still raining,' they said in unison.

'How you feelin?' she asked and Rose looked at her and Kel knew the girl had energy enough in her because though she was a long way from all right she was spoiling for a fight.

Kel poked at the fire and it was dead and she said that she would go out in the forever rising dawn to look for food and this was what she did.

Down at the water's edge Kel carried on walking to keep

the cold from her bones. Winter was not yet upon them but the temperature skirted zero in the evening and the rain had kept everything sponged wet and wintry. The rain-fog bunched and bagged the bay and Kel watched the thick bilious clouds fight for space out on the horizon. Big bastards bumping and bullying into position, preparing for the attack. If things went their way, then the storm would about turn and run its mouth off someplace else. Leave them to fish and fend and turn their world back into being without the added wrath, give them a shot at survival. The rain was one thing, but gales were another. She wondered how much of another storm they could take.

Kel scanned the grey-slap sand for a stick. She crouched to pick the straightest and she took her knife from her belt and set to work at skinning the knots and turns from the twist of wood until it came halfway to representing a spear. She sat with her feet sunk in a pool and the salt water licked at the cuts and splinters that muddled there and she splashed them occasionally whilst sharpening the stick into a pencil-thin tip.

When the job was done she stood and jabbed it into the air and she saw Rose was watching and she waved the spear and the girl waved back. The girl with a broken rotten leg and a death wish growing. Kel wondered if Rose had got to realising yet that her life up to that point had not been so bad after all, that the things she had wished different she now hoped to return.

Kel crossed the rocks and followed the tide to where it

drew breath at the bottom of a long, twisting sandbank. Her toes enjoyed the squelch and squeal of tarry worm-casts and the soft worn ridges and peaks of sculptured sand as she made her way out to the shallows to stand and wait. She held the spear a tip-bit out the water and she watched the water bump her knees and waited for the spiralling rings of surface water to slowly unravel so she could sink her eyes into the opaque underworld and wait for breakfast or lunch or dinner to walk her way. If down there a crab happened to wander by then she would be ready for it.

She slowed her breathing down to the occasional intake of air so that nothing moved inside or out and nothing moved for a long time. The clouds came and chucked their guts fully in a wide gash splitting and still she remained with her legs balanced just so and her back bent and breaking forward. She could feel her stomach holler for attention as the thought of food grew wild. She convinced herself that soon there would be something worth waiting for and she said this over and often until the moment came when movement came, enough movement to be of interest, and she lanced the thing dead and digging into the sand.

She bent her knees to duck fully into the milky calm and she unpicked the crab from the spear.

'Got it,' she shouted and she lifted it high into the air so Rose could see. 'Told you, dint I?' She took her time to make her way back up the beach and there was a little swagger to her.

'Shush,' whispered Rose when she was in earshot and she

told Kel to be quiet because she had just got the baby off to sleep.

Kel sat down by the fire and ignored the bit-bite mood that Rose still had nipping at her. She added more wood to the fire and set about snapping the legs from the crab and fingering what there was of good meat toward the heat.

'I've never eaten crab,' said Rose.

Kel looked up at her and frowned.

'What?' asked Rose.

'You're kiddin, int you?'

'Why would I be kidding?'

'I dunno, just bout everyone's had crab I reckon.'

'Well, I guess I'm not everyone.'

Kel pushed the meat around on the flat stone with a stick and she waited for the girl to return to a better mood.

'You probably think I ate fancy food and nothing much else before all this.'

Kel tried to ignore her, but she couldn't help but say she had never paid much mind to the lifestyle of those who lived in the towers.

'You think you're so funny, don't you, Keryn.'

'Not really.'

'You find it so easy to point a stick at what you don't know. You might just as well get your spear and dig it in deep.'

Kel sat back on her haunches and she asked the girl what had got into her.

'Nothing,' said Rose. 'There's no point saying it, anyway,

you've got an idea of me, your mind's been made up on that score from the beginning.'

Kel shrugged and she started to say that Rose had made it easy for her to draw certain conclusions but the girl was a rolling stone.

'Up in my ivory tower or whatever. I know you lot have got names for us.'

Kel nodded and said she supposed some people did.

'What name would you call me?'

Kel looked at Rose and smiled. 'Privileged.' She nodded. 'Privileged is what I'd call you.'

'And the rest.'

'I don't shout names just cus. Int got a need for trash talk till I get to know someone.' She divided the crab meat in two and put Rose's share on to a cool stone slate for eating.

'Don't you know me well enough yet?'

'For what?' Kel passed the slate.

'For your trash talk?'

Kel shook her head and said she hadn't made up her mind.

They ate the meat in silence and shared the last of the collected water and when Kel had finished eating she told Rose that she was probably the type of girl that she would never know in truth.

'What do you mean by that?'

'Spose there's things you int ready to give away.'

'You're one to talk.'

'Dint say I wasn't.'

'You with all of your mystery and secrets circling.'

Kel didn't like where the conversation was going so she asked Rose if she was missing home yet and this made the girl laugh.

'Compared to this place? Yes!'

'And your old folks, you miss em?'

Rose shrugged. She stopped and thought for a moment. 'No I don't miss them.'

'Why not?'

'Well where do I start? Evidently you know about Dad, but my mum? She had too many high hopes for me. She was always saying I could do better.'

'What's wrong with that?' asked Kel.

'Well nothing, strictly speaking, but to the trained eye you would notice that she never achieved anything for herself. Now I know where the money comes from, she must have felt guilty. It would be hard to keep a secret like that.'

Kel looked at Rose. There was something in Kel's own mind that was twisted in dilemma. She had something to tell the girl and something she didn't want to tell and it was the same thing. It was a secret and it felt wrong to keep it from her after everything that had gone between them.

'What?' asked Rose.

'What?'

'There's something you're not saying, I can see it in your eyes.'

'Nothin.'

Rose shook her head. 'I've known you long enough to figure out when you have something to say.'

Kel turned to look out to sea and Rose did the same and they both sighed in unison when they saw the dark clouds rolling towards them like boulders.

'If I tell you somethin you gotta promise to keep it to yourself.'

Rose looked around. 'Who am I going to tell, the baby?'

They both turned to the sleeping child and smiled.

'It's bout him.'

'What about him? He hasn't got a condition, has he? Your heart thing or whatever.'

Kel shook her head and said she didn't think so anyway.

'What then? What about the baby?'

Kel coughed nervously, 'There int nothin wrong with him.'

'OK.'

'And he int to blame for nothin.'

Rose laughed. 'What did he do, get in with the wrong crowd?'

'Don't joke.'

'What then? It can't be that bad.'

'It is that bad, to most anyway.' Kel looked at the baby and then she looked at Rose and she told the girl she had never told the secret before: 'I int never even said it out loud, int even put it to the wind.'

Rose hauled herself closer and she told Kel to go on.

'It's the baby's father.'

'And?'

'He int no swamp lad or whatever you might think.'

201

'That's good.'

'It int good, it's Dad.'

'What is?'

'My dad's his dad.'

Rose stared at Kel while she filtered the information down into fine logic.

'What?' she asked.

'My dad. He's the baby's father.'

'No, he isn't.'

Kel sighed and she looked away so Rose couldn't see her stupid girl tears.

'Shit,' said Rose.

Kel shrugged; she couldn't speak.

'Double shit.' Kel could see Rose wanted to know more so before she could ask Kel told her there was nothing more to say, except that whatever went on back then she'd never wanted to happen.

Rose put her hand on her shoulder and it felt wrong and Kel pushed it away.

'Sorry,' said Rose and she put her hands into the folds of her lap.

'Int your fault.'

'Well, I'm sorry anyway.'

Kel shrugged and said it didn't matter, stuff happened for happening's sake.

'Still,' said Rose, 'you're not responsible for the things that happened to you, for the stuff that happened in that shack where you were reared.'

'Sounds like I'm an animal amongst many, spose that's just about the truth of it.'

'I'm just saying, it wasn't your fault.'

'Never thought it was.'

'Well, I just mean if you're feeling guilty or whatever.'

'I int.'

Rose looked at her and Kel shrugged as a way of proof that she didn't care.

'I've seen the scars,' Rose continued. 'The scars on your arms.'

'I know where I put em.'

'Some say it's because of hatred, don't they? Hating yourself or whatever.'

Kel looked across at the girl who had unwittingly become the only person worth anything in her life and shook her head and she told her it was anger that drove her to it. 'Some days I could just pick up the world and throw it.'

'Because you hate it?'

'No, cus it hates me.'

Kel shook the tears from her eyes and she watched her friend stretch to pet the baby's head.

'At least one good thing came from the bad,' said Rose.

'What?' asked Kel. 'What's good bout abusin?'

Rose gestured toward the baby. 'Nothing good but the baby, and he's more than good.'

Kel shrugged. She wasn't so sure. The baby was a millstone weight around her neck.

'He int no good for me,' she said. 'Int no good for me and I defo int good for him.'

'Don't talk rubbish.'

'It's true though, I can't look after him right and we both know it, draggin him all round and now look where I got him.'

Rose told her to stop talking stupid talk. 'There's a reason you took him with you.'

Kel shrugged and she looked down at the sleeping boy. 'Poor bugger, he don't know nothin but milk just about.'

Rose smiled. 'At least you've stopped calling him it.'

'Spose.'

'Do you have a name for him yet?'

Kel shook her head and said she was working on it. 'Int much inspiration out here.'

The two girls looked at each other and the little something that was wired between them sparked just a little and Kel looked away.

Rose rubbed her hands to the fire and then she sat back and asked Kel if there was anything more she wanted to share.

'Bout what?'

'I don't know, what about your mother?'

'Died.'

'Did you know her?'

'Died when I was born or bit before or after. Can't remember all what I was told; kin int big on talkin up the past.'

'Do you have a big family?'

'Bigger un big, but none worth botherin to name.'

'Brothers and sisters?'

'Older just.'

Kel looked at the child, looked away. She tried to think of something interesting to say, but her life had always been dead-end and deadbeat, the same as everyone else she knew. So she looked at Rose and said she had no family except those who made her live like a slave and kept her running drugs.

'Where do they get the drugs from?'

'Home cookin.'

'And you liked doing it?'

'No.' Kel poked at the fire and arranged it better so she could keep from the guilt.

'I hope you've changed your mind about the kidnap?'

Kel smiled and said of course she had.

'Well that's good, that's one good thing to know, so thank you for that.'

'You're welcome.'

'It would be a bloody shame otherwise, to go through all this and then have to deal with that on top.'

'Spose you might think bout gettin back to a better life.'

Rose looked across at Kel and said she supposed that was the same for both of them and Kel agreed.

A new start over sounded good. It sounded good to hear someone say it and it felt good to think it over and have it settle in her mind.

Maybe someday her dream really would come true, the hill with the little cabin house and the low-level rivers running and falling tides and the sun happy in heaven.

'It would be somethin,' she said suddenly, 'to see the sun again and everythin.'

Rose agreed. 'It would just about make the start to a better life, I reckon.'

'Even just to see it proper,' Kel continued, 'for a moment even, to know it still existed. That would be somethin.'

Rose sighed. 'It would be everything.'

The two girls sat with the ice-winds rustling around them. It snapped at their exposed skin like gummy gang dogs, harmless but threatening the same.

'You hear that?' asked Kel suddenly.

'What?'

'Callin, I spose, some kind of callin.'

'Some kind of animal?'

Kel said maybe, but maybe not. She hoped it was nothing but a dumb thing with four legs scratching and a mouth with noises rattling within just because. She sat up close to the entrance of their cave and remembered the shadows that danced the day through and she moved beyond the fire and squatted in the wet sand and looked to the back of the cave and then at the sky.

'No stars,' she said. 'No stars and the storm's still circlin.' She sat with her knees pressed tight to her chin and her arms wrapped protecting and watched the ice-grit rain as it turned to hail and dug a billion craters in the sand. The strange land had become stranger still, its colour grey to blue to bright-frost white, ethereal and empty despite the crashing dangling storm.

Shapes shifted and jostled at the shoreline for a peek at her and they made hands of the wind and beckoned for her to come play, come swim with them. Kel rubbed her eyes. She knew that she should lie down and sleep, but sleep would not come. Madness had sunk in from all the bad talk and it settled within, rot and rust that came with the fog to clot and scab her usual practical thoughts. Corrosive thinking: things that weren't there before were there now.

Kel saw that Rose was bedding down to sleep and that image made her smile and she stepped fully from the cave and out into the rain and down the beach toward the shadows. She watched them skid into the rising tide as she approached. She told them whether they were listening or not that she would not break the little happiness she had been gifted. She would put it into her damaged heart and like a healing thing it would not be removed.

Chapter Twelve

It wasn't until the arrival of a new day that Kel realised she must have slept at times during the night and she was grateful for that but she was more thankful for the morning. She looked across at Rose and smiled. They were alone again, the island cleared of spirits.

'Mornin,' she said.

'Already?'

Kel nodded and she sat up and stretched to rescue the fire. 'I thought it would never come.' She bent to blow life into the embers. 'Thought I'd never see daylight again.' She added a little of the stored wood to the one good spark and blew it into life.

'I'm glad of everything,' said Rose. She went to sit up and Kel helped her and then took up the blanket and placed it lightly on the girl's lap. She was careful not to wake the baby.

Neither girl spoke about Rose's leg because it was a thing that existed and a thing they didn't want to exist. Kel kneeled her way to the entrance of the cave and she wondered which way the weather might go.

'It's not so bad out there, is it?' asked Rose. 'it sounds like the wind and the rain have gone.'

'They'll be back.' Kel tried to follow the thickening clouds that assembled out on the horizon but they had a toe in both directions.

She stood up and left the cave and looked out at their surroundings; both the beach and the sea wore the same cloak as yesterday. When Rose asked what she was thinking she said she was thinking about food. Her eyes were on the dolphin and she watched the gulls make good work at pecking holes in its hide. She wondered what it would taste like and she wondered about it out loud.

'I'm not eating any dolphins,' said Rose and when Kel looked down at her she shook her head and repeated her words.

'Won't it be just like shark?' asked Kel.

'I'm not eating any sharks either.'

'But folks do, don't they? Shark steaks or whatever.'

'You tell me, you're the one from the swamps.'

Kel took her knife from its sheath and passed it from hand to hand. What harm could it do? It was energy, and Kel needed that today in order to climb the cliff and work on the rescue fire. The animal was already dead and with the slamming waves and the gulls gone crazy it was a hundred times dead. She set off down the beach and she heard Rose shout that she would rather starve than eat the goddamn dolphin but Kel ignored her. If she did not provide them with more food that was just what would happen, and she knew without doubt that starvation on the island would be long-drawn and spirit-infected.

She went on toward the animal; even when the stench of putrid flesh caught hook-like in her throat and threatened to haul out what little content lay in her gut, she went on.

Her eyes searched between the patches of rip and tear for clean meat. The dolphin was no more animal than it was a factory carcass, clubbed and chopped. A thing that had no purpose beyond feeding the island's wretched inhabitants. She bent to it and settled her knees in the rock pool's wet and tarry grove and set about her work.

Nothing stopped the girl from digging. Knife in hand, she stabbed and levered the thick-leathered blubber into sizeable chunks, and even when the seagulls came back fighting and clawing she did not stop until her shirt that she had laid out for collecting the bounty was sack full. She gathered the cloth and tied the sleeves to corners and it was a beast in itself that she carried across her shoulders and back up the beach.

'It's good food,' she said to Rose as she dropped the bundle at the entrance of the cave. 'Good food goin to waste.'

Rose sat forward and sniffed at the thing in the flannel sack. 'How are you going to cook it?' she asked.

Kel shrugged and wondered if it was steak or fish or what was it? She sat beside her haul and a bit of pride and a bit of shame fought amongst themselves within her.

'I'm gonna smoke it,' she said suddenly.

'Smoked dolphin?'

Kel got up and nodded and she went about finding damp green sticks in which to trap the meat. If she smoked the flesh they would have food for a long time to come. She told herself they wouldn't need it, but just in case, it was good to be prepared.

She scrambled a little way up the cliff and cut and pulled the new shoot roots from the slate-slip earth and felt them for bend and they were good. Kel Crow had an idea and nothing would stop her now. They would sleep well with the fire raging and smoking through the day and night and in the morning they would eat like kings.

She brought the sticks back to the cave and all through the day she wove them as best she could into open-book racks, one and two, and when the racks were secured to two hands holding she set about cutting the chunks of meat into thin slices.

Occasionally she caught Rose watching and Kel would smile the awkward out of her because she could not let the girl know that she was feeling anything other. What it was to feel every emotion just from looking. It made her mad and she put her back into the chopping. To look too long was to be close to shouting crazy from the island summit: the girl had her and she had her so completely it broke her to think that Rose might die because if Rose died then Kel would die the same. Without her knowing it Rose had reached into her chest and found Kel's heart; it was in her hands now.

'You know it's dead already, don't you,' said Rose and Kel ignored her. 'It had better taste nice, what with all the effort you're putting into it.'

'It'll taste what it tastes; it's the goodness I'm after.' She laid the strips in neat rows up and down one side of her contraption and secured them into place with the other and then she poked the tripod points that she had secured above the fire clean through it.

'There,' she nodded when she had finished and stepped back. 'I did it.' She glanced over at Rose in the hope of a little praise, but the girl had gone back to sleep.

Kel sat with her feet to the fire and she stretched her legs to the heat to have it dry her jeans. Occasionally she found herself watching Rose and she wished she knew something of the girl's heart to know her completely. The firefly flutter that seared within scared Kel; it had her blood run hot with hope and cold with the fear of loss and these feelings were new to her and not just new but so unexpected that they had her whispering to the island spirits for advice.

When night came she curled up close to the fire with her eyes full of beauty and the thought of everything that was good firing her through. When sleep came it carried with it hope and it was as if everything from thereon in would be better than before.

The next morning they ate some of the meat without discussion and Kel told Rose that she was going back up the cliff. Energy and thinking had returned and she reached into her pocket, found her notebook and pencil and wrote

'RESCUE FIRE' beneath her new plan. It was obvious, she wondered why she hadn't thought of it before.

When Rose asked to see what she had written Kel passed it to her.

'Rescue fire?' she asked.

'That's right.'

'Have you seen a ship?' asked Rose. 'I mean, since we've been here?'

Kel thought for a minute; she knew where this was going. 'No, but –'

'So why are you bothering to spend precious energy on it?'

Kel shook her head. 'Cus it's all I got.' She waited for Rose to hand back her notebook, watched her flick through all her past plans.

'Always planning,' Rose said. 'Always running after something.'

'Or runnin from,' said Kel.

'That's funny. You've written "Operation" here, but after that ...'

'What?'

'Nothing. You've left it blank.' Rose looked up at Kel. 'What comes after?'

Kel shook her head. 'I don't know.' This was a lie. She did know. It was freedom.

When Rose handed back the notebook Kel went and stood at the foot of the cliffs and waited for the best part of the day to stretch out in front of her and the worst to bunch behind. She kicked at the roots that had fallen and died and she thought about the night spirits and it felt good to be certain in regard to things again. She wasn't mad, just had moments of lunacy, and she knew it was the continued hunger and sleep deprivation that had overtaken her. She would storm the cliff once more and light herself a huge bonfire piled ten foot high with all the wet roots and green wood timber she could find. Day or night, if a ship passed by the island they would see smoke or flames, they would see her fire. Things would get back on track and it started with the one-foot two-foot mountain stab.

This time it was a little easier. She found that she had scratched divots into the surface where on day one she had toed the near impenetrable earth, and so she followed her previous route with a spider's stick and crawl. She would defeat the crumbling ice-island, keep chipping at it until its back was broken in two.

The cliffs were hers and so was the island no matter how hard her heart beat and punched in her chest, and she ignored it and kept on at the kick and climb until she reached the summit.

She lay on her back to enjoy the one-minute wonder of light that had appeared briefly through the dull day. Through the circle of blue she could see the thin puff tail of an aeroplane and it startled her to see the world still pushing on. The rich still got to do as they pleased and she supposed the poor still got to dream on from the gutters that surrounded the new world walls. For a moment she thought about Dad and the brothers and sisters and kids born or bought and all bred

214

the same out there in the swamp woods, and she wondered about them enough to have a little sickness rise in her throat and she coughed and spat it into the wind. She promised herself that nothing would turn her from the job of salvation, no matter how the voices of memory shouted her down to a worthless nub.

She set to work scouting any wood not fixed down and dragged it close to the cliff edge and she set about lighting the fire with the twist of tinder bundled in her pocket and the small flame soon grew into a big damp fire that was smoking up a storm, a forever fire that meant rescue.

She found a rock for sitting and leaned back with her wrists resting on her knees. She let the heat flush her cheeks and hands and the skin that showed through the holes in her jeans. Her eyes followed the scribble-tail scars that dented her arms to mess and for the first time in memory there was no part of her that wanted to do damage, and with that thought she moved forward and blew into the fire. This was it; this was the fire that would free them from the island. The fire that would send out smoke signals high and far above the sea and bring in a boat that was good-folk and not pirates and maybe it was fairytale but it was all Kel had.

At times she used a scramble of dead bracken to stop and start the smoke and when the rain returned and the wind picked up she used both to her advantage until the island peak was nothing but blinding acridity.

When dusk fell Kel made more of the flames and she fanned them almost out of control, using fire and heat to push back the wet that came and kept coming and the damn pushy wind.

All evening long Kel held on to the glimmer of light that was the fire.

She had made a promise to herself to keep it alive, because that life meant *they* had a chance of living too, but as the rain grew heavier, the wind caught the droplets of water and blew them into every corner of the fire. When the colour faded and black ember soot began pooling there she continued to talk it through to something. She sat in the black and pulled good wood from the sop and she searched the wreckage for signs of life but finally there were none. The fire had gone out, gone and taken with it the last of the light from the sky and the only spark Kel had been carrying inside, her star of hope snuffed out.

It was a dark night. For all the nights that had come and gone, it was the darkest night.

She bunched her knees to her chest and watched the darkest clouds move out to sea and she let the last of the rain soak her complete and she bent forward to let it tip from her head. Beyond the drum and roll of wind running riot she could hear her name come calling. She told herself it was nothing more than the stirring island spirits. She closed her eyes to the night because it was all black in any case and cupped her hands to her ears for quiet. Inside her fortress she could hear the run-rabbit beat of her heart and its rhythm was the discord of a wrong song and flanking it beside she heard her name again and she recognised the voice; it was the voice of her father, thick through with the tone that meant business. He had come to get her.

Kel shook her head to loosen what she knew was her memory playing tricks, but still she kept herself in hiding the way she always had. A little girl so tiny in size and might, she knew all the cracks and splits in the shack and every hiding place she made her own, no matter that most were passed to her from her sisters like hand-me-downs. But the little girl still got got either way, and then down on to the bed and deeper down toward the dark and the night that went on for days.

All of a sudden the fight that had been in her since childhood was everywhere. The anger that burnt hot like flame-gas lifted in her and she squeezed her head to popping to stop the expanding bloat, but there was only one way to stop the explosion and that was to leach the steam from her flesh.

It was then that Kel took the knife from her belt and she lifted her shirtsleeve and pressed it into her arm and with one flash she swiped the blade in deep.

The colours that came with the release were everything that was rainbow in her mind. Kel breathed them in, she could smell them and taste them on her tongue. Every flavour was beyond memory. They belonged to another place and it was a good settling place, a place of such tranquillity, except it didn't last. The pallid hue of real life soon returned. Black nothing and then white surf something coming and going in the cove below, the sea just being, beating.

She stood and turned an ear, let the rumble of turning water take over and wash her thinking clean. She was either

217

overthinking things or she was not thinking things through enough, and both directions had the potential for losing grip. Reality was, then it wasn't, and then what was it? Since falling prey to the island Kel's imagination had her tricked into all kinds of thinking.

She looked down toward the subsiding cliffs as they scrambled into the night sky. She could hear the scuff of falling, slipping slate-stones, and suddenly she saw one solitary light swinging like a fluttering firefly in the white-caps below. Kel knew it was nothing, just her mind playing tricks, but still, it got to her.

'What you want?' she shouted and she waited for an answer and when none came she threatened whatever it was out rattling that she was not one to be shaken, and she looked around her but all she could see was four hoary steel walls surrounding her. Whether sky or sea or cliff face the island had become their prison. It had captured them and beaten them, and now came madness, and madness was the worst of all.

Chapter Thirteen

Kel lay down in the remnants of happy-maybe and the smell of wet burnt sod was the smell of death. She closed her eyes and held her breath, waited for her heart to slow, tap out. If it wasn't for the thought of the girl waiting for her down by the beach and the baby that was her charge she might have remained, waited until the spirits decided to take her. But thinking about Rose had Kel picturing her smile and the beauty that radiated there.

Kel wanted her to smile again, pink cheeked, to get her back to some shade of beauty. If Kel helped Rose to find that old self then she would also help herself. To care for another was to care for all humankind; the tip-turned society was a mess worth fighting for after all. If Kel could only come good, then the world would spin back strong and caring.

She kicked off toward the cliff edge and in the pitch black she felt around for the dip in the ledge for the descent, but with every step the earth gave way. The cliff had become the foundation for a waterfall; turned the island's mud and guts into a river riding out to sea. Whatever rough-route path Kel had tried to follow in her ascent was long gone now. She would have to find another way down, head instead toward the cove where she had first found Rose and the baby.

The storm had lessened a little, and occasionally the moon found a way through the clouds enough to offer guidance and Kel took it. She took to running across the island plateau and when a spiteful rock or root put out to trip her up she got back to her knees and then to her feet. She did not stop until she was at the other side of the island, where the descent was an every-day walk down toward the beach. Kel could feel her heart pump hard and fast in her chest and she pleaded for it to not give up on her now. She could feel it ballooning up against all else, a thick-skinned pig ball bullying her ribs into snap-sticks. An organ too big even for a giant. She put her hands to her chest and hugged it in, told it to stay put, be good, beat strong.

She traipsed the divide of wet dragging sand until she could no longer walk and then she stood and waited until the moon silvered the sea so she could gauge the tide in its comings and goings. Given up but with her instinct for going on, Kel made one more lap around the cove and that was when she saw it: sticking out of the mud-bank cliff like a marker to a past life was the stolen day-glo oar. Poking from the island in a last-ditch attempt at being saved.

She ran toward it and pulled the oar from the sand with a cheer. A new plan of rescue came into her head and it was better than the last. She could do it and she would do it.

Kel sat on the sand and thought. She would build a boat, a raft, a floating jetty of flotsam to sail back out to sea. All in it wasn't about being rescued, it was about rescuing yourself.

That was something worth thinking about and she lay on the beach and planned everything out of her system until she was left with a good-to-go floating water craft of her imagination.

All the useless rubbish that had beached on the shore near their cave in the storms had the potential for use, she realised. The drum containers and the squares of polystyrene. Plastic crap that had journeyed wrong into the ocean and had travelled up and down the forever shores to become something right.

Kel would make use of them, breathe new life into the dead cells with knots and prayers.

Kel sat at the edge of the shoreline and waited for the dawn to come and pull the tide closer and put a little light into the sky. She would have to wait and watch for the thin pewter strands of low-tide water to cover the horizon like lucky streams. When the time was right for swimming depths she would jump right in, swim the bay with the oar across her back and get back to Rose and the baby and the bit-bob flotsam. Then she could set about making the raft.

When the tide grew high she walked the surf and washed the blood from her arm and then she went into the sea fully with the soak riding past her knees. When the light was halfway good she etched out a route in her mind's eye and she took it.

Since the last storm, the sea had returned to sub-zero sucking and Kel could imagine ice-crystals clutching and worming into the seams of her jeans. But still she went on, and when she could no longer feel anything of herself and her legs dangled like blubber-babies she swam on with her head out of the water so her brain would not freeze. She swam hard with the ice-soup tugging her backwards and the oar passing from one hand to the other, and she clawed at the water and kicked her way free of its grasp. Fighting her way towards the jut of cliff-rock that separated the two bays was all she could think about, and she knew that with her strange heart beating somewhere within her numb chest she would soon set foot on to the beach and into a new day. Occasionally she caught a current that floated her toward her destination and this was how she finally crashed in.

'Rose,' she shouted as she headed up the beach and she squinted for fire or movement or both.

'Rose?' Kel stood at the entrance of the cave and she said the girl's name over and she kicked into the embers of the fire for the light and she saw the baby in its makeshift bed and she bent to check for breathing.

Dawn was breaking. It snapped and cracked above her head and it drew her attention back out toward the ragged rip-line water.

Kel adjusted her eyes to the new morning light and that was when she saw her, a dark shape shifting in the tide.

'Rose,' she shouted and she ran back down the beach toward the slumped figure and pulled her from the wet. 'What you doin?'

'I'm cleaning myself,' said the girl, and she looked up at Kel with eyes full and flashing mad with ocean colours.

'What you talkin bout?'

'My leg.' Rose bent to the salt water and splashed it over the wound.

'You're crazy,' said Kel.

'I know.'

'Crazy slippin and slidin all ways to get here. Let me carry you back to the cave.'

'In a bit, I've not finished cleaning.'

Kel looked down at Rose's half-rotten leg beneath the sink of water. She wished there was a way to clean it properly but there was not. She put an arm around Rose and lifted her for the carry but she lay loose as a bag of compost, blood and bone.

'Put me down,' Rose shouted. 'Put me down, Kel, I've not finished, I can still smell the rot in my leg.'

'Don't be daft, it's just its way of healin,' Kel lied. She had caught it too; the high-fly stench of festering flesh fizzed at the tip of her tongue and stitched the back of her throat shut.

Kel lay Rose at the mouth of the cave and sat down beside her. They sat in silence for the longest time and watched the sky brighten and then Kel told her about the plan to make them a raft.

Rose looked around at the beach and said she wondered if what had happened before might happen again.

'What you mean?' asked Kel.

'We might capsize.'

Kel shrugged and said she would have a good go at it in any case. 'Either the storm gets us or it don't, we'll just have to take our chances is all.'

'What about getting rescued?'

'You were right.' Kel looked at Rose. 'We int gettin rescued, we're goin to have to rescue ourselves.' She stood up and looked at the plastic barrels that were strewn up and down the beach and she looked back at the girl and told her things would work out all right.

'Do you promise?'

Kel sighed and promised something more than nothing. She could see tears pool in Rose's eyes as they reflected the morning light.

'For all my partying, all the drinking and the laughter, did you know I wanted to die?'

Kel shook her head.

'Before all this. I wanted to die just because I didn't want to live.'

'When?' asked Kel.

'Back home. Before the ship and everything that happened.'

Kel looked away because she didn't know what to say.

'I don't want to die any more, Kel, don't you think that's funny?'

Kel looked at her and shrugged. It wasn't so funny. She had known people with their heads half-in and half-out of happy, and she thought about herself and the harming and what folks mistook as misery. It wasn't misery; it was anger.

'Because when I had everything,' Rose continued, 'and there wasn't any danger, I thought that danger was what I wanted. But now here I am, practically waist-deep in my grave and I don't want it so much any more.'

Kel smiled and told her the best thing she could do for hope and happiness right then and there was rest.

'I want to live, Kel, more than anything I want to live.' Tears were smearing up Rose's face and still Kel saw beauty there.

'I'm gonna get us off this island,' Kel said suddenly. 'Off the island and off the bastard sea and put us somewhere back to safe and solid.'

At once Kel set about collecting everything that was not sand from the beach and she was determined to make use of it all. She would build a craft worthy of the three of them and worthy of everything the sea and sky had to offer. She would work the day through from one end to the other to keep the thought of Rose from her mind. She lay the plastic containers in a line on the sand and there were four of them. That would be the base. Four empty barrels and all with their waterproof caps intact.

Kel could not find words to describe some of the plastic jumble junk. Broken objects split and rounded by the bash and smash of rocks and water, and each thing gummed with tar and oil. Objects that had gone around the world and would go around the world again.

She found a net more string than rope that had caught between the teeth of tumbling boulders and she unpicked it and wound the good strands between her hand and arm. When the rope ended she added more with a good double knot, and this she plaited and used to tighten the barrels together and she did the same with the bits of misshapen wood.

All day through Kel worked on the raft despite the usual ice-rain weighing her down, and she was able to win over her heart that was close to ripping by fuelling it with hope. Kel Crow would save Rose's life and by doing so she would save her own.

Not just save it but shake it up and change it, make good from all that was bad. Kel looked over at Rose to see if she had seen the raft taking shape, but the girl was sleeping and she looked at the bit-bob pile of rubbish she'd collected and wondered what was best for making a spare paddle. A plank of wood with the weight of the world stained into its grain, or a half-scooped two-litre milk carton? She told herself to leave nothing to chance. The thought of being without any kind of paddle or oar still stuck in her memory like a bone lodged in the throat. Two paddles were better than one, nothing was going to stop them this time. She sat astride her beached vessel with her legs dangling and going over her options, going over every potential danger that might catch them out in the dark and the wet and the constant storms that rattled continually. She thought back to the night they capsized. If there were things she could have done better she would think them through now; stupidity was in the past, along with green-gills and a plain old hope in things turning right.

Preparation was everything, so she packed a hundred days of thinking into the one day and then she looked out to sea. She could feel the blue-grey reflecting in her dark eyes, its spirit pushing at her, and Kel pushed back.

When there was nothing more to be done to the boat besides fancy, Kel roped it and dragged it down to the shore. She watched to see how it floated as the sea gathered it into its arms. In coming days it would become bed and home and shelter, a place for living out their last days on earth or their first few days of a new life.

Kel pushed the raft further out into the sea and she looked at the moody sky that refused to show the sun and she rough-guessed its whereabouts anyway.

She looked ahead and thought about where they should head for once they were waterborne once more. She found the sun and worked out which was west because that was where the sun was already beginning to set, and she knew that this island could only be south of the mainland. So they would have to head north. Because if the route they'd followed onboard Rose's dad's ship went one way and the route they had unfollowed on the life raft went another, then there was only one way back on track open to them. They would have to retrace their footstep-seasteps until they crossed the shipping lane, hang out in the strait and hope good followed bad.

She leaned on to the raft and lifted her legs out of the

water to test the bounce, and when it didn't sink she jumped up on to her stomach and lay flat with her breath held tight until she could trust the platform to not capsize. Kel sat up and settled the oar in the water to steady herself. She let out a little breath, and then a little more, and then she put a hand against her heart and came close to uttering a promise-prayer that said something about doing the best she could. She dug the oar into the sea occasionally and she lifted the water and watched it trickle over the ridges of plastic.

She wished she'd had the foresight to build the boat when first they had smashed into the island, but back then seemed like a hundred days in the past. Time was a stop-start carry on anyway. Since the *Kethovek* it had developed parallel zones and realities and there had been moments after the boat capsized that it stopped altogether. Minutes had become hours and hours became a lifetime of cold black night.

Kel took the vessel as far as she dared and she marked the ridge of rock that surrounded their cove and she told herself yes, it was doable. They were stubborn rocks, but together they would leave the island tomorrow for good.

Back on the beach she pulled the boat a little way out of the water and she tied some of the netting rope she had found earlier to the bow of the boat and secured the other end to a rock that protruded from the sand and she tied it tight until there was no rope left to knot and she went to sit by Rose who had woken recent.

'There's a few winkles if you want them,' said Rose, and she passed Kel a fistful of wet chew.

'Thanks.' Kel put one in her mouth and swallowed it down with a gulp of water.

'So?' Rose asked.

'What?'

'How's the raft coming along?'

'It's good,' she said. 'It works.' She looked at Rose and told her about the ring of rocks that circled their bay.

'Can you get past it with me in the raft if it's mostly rock? You struggled to float just me around those rock pools.'

'It'll work, it has to.'

Kel picked up the baby and she sat him in her lap for his feed. 'Won't be long now,' she told him. It would not be long until they were freed from the island shackles; freed and rescued and saved good and proper.

She petted the baby's head and held him up so she could look into his eyes. What it was to be innocent and without worry, an eager face and untarnished spirit ready to take on the world. He started to cry and she passed him over to Rose for the calm.

Tomorrow they would win this game called life. At first light they would be up and out and off; packed and settled on the raft and heading out toward the sea. Once more upon the deep unfathomable blue, not quite back on track but heading somewhere other.

Chapter Fourteen

Kel couldn't recall when it was that the bit-bad and unusual weather upgraded itself into the next category of storm. She lay in the cavity that was nestled between sleep and awake and listened to the roaring waves. She told herself it was just a dream, it had to be. She opened her eyes and sat up straight, felt the fear creep up her spine and sit heavy across her shoulders. At the mouth of the cave she could see the top layer of sand had been lifted by the wind and it blew across the beach and made dunes of the rocks. The tide had changed too, giant waves heaved from the ocean floor and crashed against the shoreline.

Kel looked across the fire toward Rose, and when she saw that the girl was still sleeping she crept from the cave. To know the storm fully was to put them someplace within it; to have the hammer fall or keep it firmly in hand.

Kel stood with the world hurtling towards her and she shielded her eyes from the torrent to focus on what the dawn light cared to show and she looked for the raft. She ran down the stubby thin-strip of sand toward the place where she had anchored it yesterday but found the rock was buried in shifted sand, whilst the raft had completely disappeared. She fell to her knees and dug her hands into the sand but it was no use, the vessel she had so lovingly constructed was gone.

Kel waded into the grappling surf and peered east to where the early morning light revealed all in its pointing and she saw fully what destruction the night's run-river rain had caused. The cliff that was once a clean cake-slice of rock was nothing now but a mountain of silt and tumble stones falling into the rolling waves. It was as if the island was melting and with it Kel and Rose and the baby were dissolving the same. She wrapped her arms around herself in some pretence of normality and looked toward the cave. This was where they lived. A cavity cut into the earth, a triple grave. The raft that was going to save them and bring them back toward the living was gone and it was gone good. No matter how far she dared to step into the surf and stretched herself to peer toward the other bay, nothing but a great big barrel of empty glared back.

Kel knew even before the thumping waves tripped her that she should turn back, but the image of the raft was scratched so mighty in her mind that she could see it and see it and see it. She could see the raft in her mind and she felt like it was in reach and so she stretched and paddled and then she swam. When her feet were swept clean of any grounding and a little salt water sloshed in her gut, Kel finally turned into the waves and she let them pick and tip her and return her to the shore.

She lay in the encroaching tide, heavy rain making pools of her eyes and she emptied herself fully of care. The island would not let her go; suddenly Kel knew this without any doubt. It was as if she were paralysed both inside and out. Everything had stopped and was broken and gone.

She could hear Rose calling out and she wondered what she might say to her to make all the wrong partway right. If there were one right thing to say that would have her grasp hold of hope then Kel would think it and say it, but all faith was lost.

She reached for her notebook and threw it into the sea. No more dreams, no more plans worth making.

Kel looked to where Rose was huddled in the cave with the screaming baby and she got up with the crazy wind pushing her every which way and she went to them. She did not speak and she picked up the boy and they watched as he sucked the last bit of strength from her.

Kel thought about what it must be like for him. To be oblivious to the wilds, unaware of the weather in all its extremities and the ravishing hunger that was twisting her belly down to a bud. She doubted if he even heard the island's noise in its proper form, the constant forever running wind that had burrowed its way into her ears and threatened to live there always, minute after hour after every day. She looked up from the baby to see Rose's eyes set on her and Kel asked her what it was she wanted her to say.

'Something,' said Rose simply, her eyes filling with tears. 'Something more than nothing.'

Just then they heard movement above their heads, a shifting of earth and rock, they could see it tumble at the mouth of the cave. It fell like a waterfall.

Kel shoved the baby into Rose's arms.

'I can't believe this is happenin,' she said. One thing after another, the island did not want them to leave. She looked at Rose and shook her head and all she could think to say was *game over*, so she kept her words to herself. She was all out of ideas, empty of any notion and thought besides dying. She went tentatively toward where the mouth of the cave used to be and put her hands against the rocks that had fallen there, her fingers gripped, pulling but nothing fell loose.

'We're trapped.' Kel turned to Rose and looked at her through the dim light. 'There int no way back.'

'You can't give up on us,' said Rose.

Kel cleared her throat. 'I int,' she lied, and she reached for the baby and put him on her shoulder.

'There's a sliver of light at the top,' said Rose. 'You could try and push through.'

'Dint you hear me? We're trapped, buried alive.' Kel could feel the surge of panic rising in her, an ocean rushing, and she turned her head into the baby's; to smell him and feel his warm cheek on hers was to keep the fear at bay one minute longer. She thought she could hear his heartbeat, hear her own. The sudden silence that ballooned within the cave was the worst kind of noise, it was everywhere, went nowhere.

The cave was a death knell; it smelt of the damp cliff, wet smoke, dead things.

Kel sank to the floor of the cave and closed her eyes and hid down deep in that well of despair. She could hear Rose's voice and felt her hand on her leg, but all things that were love and comfort were a million miles from Kel now and when the baby started to cry Rose took him from her and Kel dropped into the space where he had been. If ever there was uncharted land, then this was it; a world where Kel did not belong.

In the little light that remained in the cave Kel watched as Rose settled the baby to some level of sleep before coming to lie near and Kel let the girl stretch to her and put her arms around her.

Rose told her it was going to be all right and she lifted Kel's face to look at her and she repeated what she said.

Kel looked into her eyes and that was when she fell head first. She couldn't speak, and didn't know what to say even if she could. Her words clogged the back of her throat and sat fat and larded on her tongue. It was as if everything that had been inside her now lay strewn all around them; her life chewed over and spat out and stamped to dust.

Rose continued to talk. 'I'm just telling you what you've been telling me all along.' She wiped Kel's face with the corner of some rag and it was a surprise to both of them to see tears there.

'You're daft, do you know that?' said Rose. 'Daft, for all your tough ways.'

Kel tried to laugh.

'It's true. I know more about you than you know yourself.'

Kel doubted it and she looked away with shame, and when Rose tilted her head back to look at her again she felt a hundred times shame for the things she had done.

The two girls looked at each other for what seemed like forever and when Rose leaned close to kiss her it was the only thing left to do in the world that made any kind of sense.

Kel felt the loose detritus that had fallen from her beginning to rebuild, and where it stacked back up it felt twice tougher than before. Rose breathed life into her as they kissed, and they held each other close until the day became night became day again.

Neither girl spoke to keep the moment complete and Kel was grateful for the small mercy that was the world standing still for them. A moment's peace and a moment's grace in which to become themselves once more. She pushed Rose from her just a little to see her face in the falling firelight and she told her she was sorry for the kidnap, that she was not just sorry but a hundred times sorry.

Rose smiled. 'I know,' she said simply.

'If I'd known how things would turn out, thought bout what it was I was doin, I dunno.'

Rose put a finger to Kel's lips. 'It doesn't matter now,' she said. 'It doesn't matter because here we are, and everything good has been swapped for bad and everything bad has been swapped for good. Everything has been equalled out.'

Kel started to laugh. 'That's a funny way of lookin at it.'

'I'm, right though, aren't I. Something good has come out of this.'

Kel nodded and she realised that what had developed between them was not just good but everything that was great and growing.

She didn't know what to say and she kept her head lowered to hide the hot burn-bubble that was coming into her cheeks. She wanted to sing out for the happy and cry for the misery that was the island and the corpses they were becoming. Everything had arrived too late, and that was the story of her life.

Kel sat up and she couldn't help but look at Rose some more for the picture she painted. Through her eyes Kel set a home fire hearth burning for the both of them and its brightness fuelled the future bright the same. She realised that Rose was home to her. She was the home that Kel had never known, and maybe there was a life worth living out there for them, a place beyond the swamps and too far away from the ocean for anything except glimpsing it in the disance.

She wanted to know 'what now', and was about to ask out loud when Rose answered her with a smile. 'We're going to get off the island.' Rose nodded. 'Get off the island and back to a life worth living.'

Rose's words were like a jab of fresh blood thinking. There had to be another way off the island, there just had to be. She turned to look at the rear of the cave and saw that a little of the slate-rock had fallen away.

'That's it!' she shouted.

She went to the back of the cave and she peered into the hole that bored high and deep into the rock. She closed her eyes and felt a little breeze against her cheek and it made her smile. Everything that wasn't then was again and the possibilities for surviving were endless and Kel wondered if the island held the puzzle-piece to living.

'What can you see back there?' asked Rose.

'The cave, it goes on forever.' Kel stretched to hold the lighter and she strained so as to see fully into the crack and she watched the flame dance in the wind as the light fanned out into the wide cavernous room.

'It's big,' she said and she turned to look at Rose, 'bigger than you'd think.'

'How big?'

'Forever big. Makes you wonder how the island stays up.'

'Well it might not stay up for much longer. Half of it's been dumped in the sea since last night.'

Kel sat down by the fire and she checked over the torches she had been making in the evenings with tar and rags.

'Do you honestly think those rags are going to hold up?' asked Rose. 'Whilst all the while we go down and through and miraculously pop out somewhere else? Are you mad?'

Kel didn't know what to say. It was better than nothing.

'If you ask me those rags won't hold up,' Rose continued. 'But I suppose it's worth trying.'

Kel nodded. She had been planning and thinking and it had all come down to this. She'd been preparing for some- thing completely different, but now this moment was upon her she found she was prepared for it all the same. They had torches for finding a way and food for eating and sticks for supporting Rose, they could do it. She packed up everything worth bothering about, including the smoked dolphin, and nothing Rose might have said in way of caution would have made any difference to her. All they could hope for was that the tunnel through the cave led somewhere and that somewhere was outside. Kel splintered and rebandaged Rose's leg to a position worthy of straight and standing and this was how she guided her into the cavity at the back of the cave. When Rose was through Kel passed her the baby and pushed through the bag of stuff and threw in the torches and she followed with a leap of faith because that was what it was, a leap and a jump and a stumble into the unknown. Inside the new gape of rock Kel lit the torch and they stood like trespassers in an alien world, the dripping fungal walls and the smell of dead sea things strangling their throats. A screw-hole in the earth that had been sculpted by the scratching ocean.

Kel looked at Rose and she saw the fear that was never far from either of them return and she took her hand, jostled the baby central in the knotted sack on her back and held the torch out in front of her to see the winding pathway in front of them. 'Let's go.'

Kel made sure to keep some light stretched above their heads to watch for falling stalactites loosened by the storm and she took her time to step further into this new world.

'Shouldn't be long,' she told herself, 'wherever it leads.

The island's only small, we swam halfway round it gettin here and that dint take so long.'

'It isn't as simple going underground though, is it?' said Rose. 'Not so simple if we end up heading at all angles. And we don't know if it goes all ways through, do we.'

Kel ignored her and she continued on the thin winding and only route available to them. To think about a path that went nowhere would have been to think about a world without hope and this was her only hope; it would work because it had to.

Occasionally the path became so thin that it was nothing more than a string line for drawing, and it was during these times that Kel had to settle the baby into a push-dip in the bag on the ground and help Rose circumnavigate the steep, unforgiving gorge. They went slow and that was fine, because time did not matter now in any case. It had given up on them a long time ago. Not since the first day that Kel had woken on the island had she seen a full morning or night; every one was cut into and cut through with a stony stab of grey. So they went on and when the path widened they stopped to fill their lungs with the breath space it afforded them, a room within a room in which to stretch the confining rock walls from their bones.

'How you doin?' Kel held the torch between them and they stood in the circle of light like holy men.

'I've been better.'

'How much walkin you got left in your legs?'

Rose shrugged. 'As much as it takes. We're halfway aren't

239

we? Seems to me like it's cutting clean through the island.' She put the sticks she'd been using to walk down on to the floor so she could flex her hands.

Kel nodded yes and inside she hoped to all the island spirits that they were right. 'You ready to push on?'

Rose didn't speak. Instead she jostled the bag on to her back and picked up the sticks and the two girls set off once more.

There were times when Kel thought she saw light up ahead and she shielded her torch, and what was there wasn't and what wasn't was. Firefly flashes of faith for the living. She wanted to tell Rose what she had seen, but the ticking time bomb that was madness was not quite for sharing and the light might have been nothing more than reflection from the one in her own hand. So she kept quiet and even when the light grew larger she kept her eyes from it.

'Kel?' asked Rose suddenly. 'Do you see what I see?'

They both stopped and looked on toward the bright, welcoming circle of brightness.

'Is there somebody up ahead do you think?' Rose shuffled forward a little. 'Has somebody got a fire going?' She giggled as she said it and Kel knew it was because the thought of other people being here all along was madness.

'Good big fire if they do.' Kel thought about the spirits and she started to laugh.

'Then what is it?'

Kel thought for a moment. 'Looks like sunlight.'

Rose stood close and looked straight into her eyes. 'Do you think?'

Kel shook her head. 'Can't be.'

'Why not?'

'We int gone further than the middle of an island.' She bent to look up toward the radiant amber light. 'Besides, we int seen proper sun in forever.'

Kel watched Rose limp and shuffle forward and she followed. Slow laboured steps towards the thing of beauty that had her scared the most. She watched as Rose's hair came back to life with golden hues reflecting, and all around them colours came and permeated everything that had not known colour before. It was as if they had found the centre of the island and the centre of the earth combined, a circle of heaven buried within the circle of hell. In Kel's mind the enclosure was what a garden might look like; it was full of vegetation and secret sitting places.

They stood in full sunlight and tilted their faces straight up for a moment's warmth and Kel closed her eyes to let them run red. Colours were everywhere. Even the baby stretched out a plump fist full of fingers in the hope that he might catch the essence of rainbow.

'The sky is blue,' said Rose and when she looked at Kel it was as if she had asked a question.

Kel nodded and they hugged and the baby put both arms in. The storm had gone.

They rested for a time on a gathering of rocks crawling with plant life and perfect for sitting.

'It's a shame we didn't know about this place before,' said Rose. 'We might have lived in here just about.'

Kel agreed, it was an oasis of calm and beauty. She imagined that the sun always shone there, its rays dipping low and out of sight of the island's grey gravel beaches, escaping and reaching down to blossom. They warmed themselves and drank the clean rock water that sprang from the cliffs and when it was time for heading neither of them wanted to go, but what else was there. The heart of the island was a good thing and needed, but Kel knew their future did not lie there. Rose's leg was bad and getting worse; each step she took pained her close to stopping and Kel feared that once stopped she would stop for good.

They went on into the new cave crossways from the one they had exited and Kel lit a second torch for the last part of the journey. Everything was much the same. The dark saline drip of island rock was back and Kel kept the memory of pure light alive in her mind. Good had come to them when they had least expected it, and by that fact alone it would come again.

The second half of the island was easier to navigate. The path was wide despite the low smack ceiling and they walked with their backs bent and buckling. Step after step they held on to each other, and when Rose slipped Kel was there to catch her. She told her that it would not be long until they exited the island rock, that she knew it in her heart and she told herself the same thing.

Now suddenly time that had stopped mattering mattered greatly; Rose was close to forever sitting, and more than once

242

she told Kel to go on without her and to promise to love the baby and help it to have a good go at life. Kel ignored her and eventually they pushed and pulled themselves clean to popping out the other side of the stubborn island rock and back into the air.

They lay on the beach and gasped breath back into their lungs. A marathon run and a marathon won all in a moment, a heartbeat flutter no matter how it beat wrong.

Kel untied the baby from her back and placed him happy-as on her lap and that was when she saw it.

'The raft,' she shouted. 'It's the bloody raft! Maybe we int so unlucky after all.' She looked at Rose and pointed her toward the perfect fixed and bound vessel that bobbed there proud and rock-pool neat.

Rose smiled and she lay back into the sand and closed her eyes. Their final journey on the island had taken its toll on her. Kel could see it in her everything, the way she took in air, and her fingers light as feathers against the wind.

'It's time to go,' Kel said and she nodded toward the tide that was snaking its way up it to greet them.

It was time to go and it was time to go forever. Let the island be and leave it to make of itself what it wanted. It was time to go for good.

Kel looked at Rose and asked if she was ready to set sail, then she got up to pack their nothing stuff into every last rubber boat remnant they still had and she lashed these to the raft and all the plastic-bottle water she'd collected recently she balanced and knotted at every corner.

When everything was ship-shape done and dusted, Kel carried Rose to the raft that she had anchored with a boulder rope and she laid her down best she could and she cut the rope and set the oar that luckily she had remembered to tie to the vessel and set it to water. Kel kept her mind to the culvert that she knew ran gauntlet between the rocks, and she told herself she knew this enviroment well enough, this island had become more of a home than any she had known.

Seated within the dusk-dark Kel could see the island's thrust and punch against the sky, could see the spirit shadows gathering out on what was left of the slip-trip edge of the cliff. She could tell the spirits had something of a celebration whooping about them. She could hear their cat-call cries and see small spark-fires burning crazy in their eyes, mad things and madness combined, and Kel recognised that they were a part of her.

She went on with the oar lifting and pulling from the ocean and she watched the ripples catch what remained of the light and felt the raft turn stubborn from the island. The tide was coming in but the wilful boat wanted shot of land; just like Kel, it wanted to leave the devil earth behind.

Kel knew exactly what lay out to sea. Beyond the gully lay a plateau of rocks and nothing but a full tide could help them skim over and out. She looked at Rose for an opinion not her own, but the girl was gone with pain after the exertion of walking wounded and so she decided to leave her be.

Kel knew matters of life and death didn't wait for thinking time, things either were or they were not. She could either go now, with a million known risks wondering, or stay for high tide and a full moon busting out with caution. But then the spirits might just succeed in bothering her all the way toward mad, or the pumping poison in Rose's veins might put her out for the gulls.

'I'm goin,' she said to herself and she dug the oar deep into the water and spaded for all she was worth.

Chapter Fifteen

They met the tide at full depth; the watery world where they had spent so much time rose up to greet them like an old friend. Kel worked hard to keep the paddle pushed in water, the horizon her goal, every minute better than the bullying island.

Occasionally the rising moon caught in the rocks and revealed their angles; like daggers they came at them and Kel was quick to navigate the raft away.

She would row out into the darkness and back into the light, another day and a lifetime of days paddling toward the forever horizon. Kel knew now that she would never give up in this life, and if her heart granted her respite then on into the next. Kel rowed until morning. She rowed them out of trouble and she rowed them toward safety for now with a good light rising.

She told Rose they had a great deal of paddling yet to come and she told her whether she wanted to hear it or not.

'I said we still got long to go, rowin and whatever.'

'Where are we heading?' whispered Rose.

'The strait, remember? We're gonna hang out in the ocean and wait for a bigger boat to come along.' She looked at Rose's leg, 'Or maybe head to the mainland, take our chances back on land.' Kel told the girl again how she was going to get her to land in one piece one way or another, that she would be back home before long.

'What about you?' asked Rose.

Kel shrugged. 'I'll be all right.'

'What about your plan? What about your heart?'

Kel thought for a moment. The plan she had set for herself so perfectly had been taken from her ten times over but it did not bother her one bit. She told Rose not to worry about her and smiled when the girl joked that she was not worried. Kel could see she was fading fast; nothing but thin-trace pencil tracks marking her out when she used to be all about the colour.

She told Rose to sleep some and when the baby started to cry she picked him up and kissed him and he squealed with delight. Kel continued to row with the boy lying in her lap and he giggled and spluttered joy and it was as if he were the happiest child alive.

'Rosen,' she said to him, 'I'm gonna call you Rosen.' She looked into his eyes and he looked into hers the same. 'It's a good Cornish name and it's a girl's name, but I'll tell you bout the reasons when you're old enough to understand what it is to be named after beauty and courage and grit.'

Kel thought about happiness and she thought about it a good while. There had been moments during their chaotic journey when she had been close to contentment. Near enough happy in the brief moments when she did not fear for her life, when thinking was allowed. Rose had been a part of that, she was certain. She wondered what in reality the world had in store for her now, and it was with newfound optimism that she thought this. There were things she did not know but what she *did* know she took as truth above all else: she would stay straight and good of the law and would not think about her heart, except to fill it with a little hope occasionally. Life would be for living now, not for thinking and planning and worrying over, and life was not for looking back at either. She glanced across at Rose and she asked a god she did not believe in to keep her safe, please God, keep her breathing.

At certain times during the day and through the night she leaned in to listen to Rose's breaths, or else she'd rest her head briefly on Rose's stomach and take comfort in its rise and fall, the touch of another reassuring and devastating in the same moment.

'We made it past the rocks,' she told her. 'Made it past the rocks and we int never gonna see the island again.'

Kel said these words many times throughout the coming days. She said them but sometimes she didn't believe them. There were nights when she looked to the horizon and saw the dancing, goading spirits, just the same small neat figurines beckoning for her to come closer despite the million miles of sea between. Sometimes they called for her to come home, but Kel didn't have a home and so she'd shout that if they knew her then they would know this. In daylight she would convince herself that she finally had them sunk, but come night-time when the rowing became too much, there they were again, monsters in the dark.

On the final morning Kel had had a night as bad as any. She couldn't sleep for fear and she couldn't row with any great meaning because the spirits now floated and flaunted themselves on the crest of every wave. She lay on her back with the oar resting across her chest and one hand trailing the water to let her know that she was still alive. All the water bottles were gone and she wished for a little rain, enough to soften the thorns that grew tangled in her throat. She hadn't drunk in a long time, little wonder that she was seeing things more than just sea and sky. Kel could imagine her veins pumping with the salt-sap, her arteries clogged with crystals stacked close and closing; her huge heart hardening to rock salt.

She spread herself starfish and held the sides of the raft, a way of grounding, settling.

Kel missed the earth beneath her feet, no matter how sodden soft, the idea of good soil and the dewy smell of morning come good. Childhood memories, but fine ones all the same. New beginnings. All she'd ever wanted was a fresh start, the one step forward without the two steps back. She stared at the sky and checked it over for gaps in the clouds and there were none, the gloom had the sky tied corner to corner.

'Won't be long now,' she said to Rose. 'Any day now.' She looked across at the girl and she was half gone with chill and fever combined and Kel thought she said something and sat up.

'What you say?' Kel asked, and she wondered how the girl could speak without moving her lips. She sat forward and continued to stare until something soft and melting appeared on the horizon beyond Rose's head; a smudge that rubbed up and down and was everywhere.

The smudge thing melting in-out above the waves was land, and it was growing in size. Kel stumbled to her feet and she shouted for Rose to wake. She watched the smudge stretch and circle them like prey and all the time she kept up with the shouting, until the last blow filtered from her lungs and her knees gave way to buckling.

'We need to keep paddlin,' she said to baby Rosen. 'We made it, we bloody made it.' But as she watched, the mark of something more than sea dissolved into the soup-slip horizon, and then she watched it disappear completely.

Kel sat down and rubbed her eyes clear, but when she opened them everything had been clogged thick with fog.

She lay down and put her head to Rose's chest and listened for signs of life and maybe there was something and maybe there was nothing at all.

'I'm sorry for not savin you,' Kel said and she closed her eyes, and for a moment she thought maybe the girl had put a hand on her head and she took comfort in it despite knowing it was just the wet fingering damp. They would lie together at death's door and wait to be let in.

Kel allowed the ocean waves to rock her thinking silent. There was nothing to fight for and nothing to fight against. A quiet drift of motion; it was only the ocean after all. She would fall to sleep and she would die in sleep.

Time passed as it always had, with fits and starts and backward ticking. Frenzied and apathetic all the same, and still the two girls and the beautiful baby lay in the holding bay before death as they had been in life, close but not close.

Two girls unaware of anything except the long drawn-out wait. Kel was near to opening the door to doing it, the door to dying, and then she heard it. The sound of a warning horn that as good as jumped Kel from her skin and that was when she saw it, a land of sorts. Real this time, she could smell the earth, taste the wet soil on her tongue. She held the baby aloft and told him that they had done it, they had found land. She knelt beside Rose and she shook her and told her the same, and then she settled back to rowing toward the low-sling cliff beach.

As the raft drew closer Kel narrowed her eyes to the detail of things. The land was dark from constant water, and rising from the earth came smoke and it was as if the ground itself was burning, and the acrid tang cut into her throat like a blade. Maybe this was it, the end of the world, just like the old man and the pirate kids had warned her so many lives ago.

Kel tucked the baby best she could into her jacket to keep him from breathing in the toxic fumes and she kept on rowing with her eyes filtering out the smoke and suddenly she saw movement, one and two, and the people came down to the shoreline to pull them in. She called out to them and all her words came out coughed and jumbled and as she reached the beach she thanked them over until her voice gave way and it was replaced with tears so forceful she thought she might suffocate in the suck.

Kel lay on the sand with the baby gripped tight in her arms, and when somebody bent to take him she shouted them away because he belonged to her. She loved him and had protected him and to have him taken from her even momentarily would feel like forever now.

She sat up and looked to Rose and the man who carried her from the raft and she shouted for him not to hurt her, she was all she had in the world besides the baby.

The man stopped a moment and looked at Kel, his arms cradled loose with the little dangling light weight in his arms, and he nodded, smiled.

'You hear me?' she shouted again. 'She needs medical attention. Don't go dumpin her in the sand.' She got to her feet and shuffled towards them and she told him the girl's name was Rose and that she had money to pay for what was needed.

The man carried Rose to the slipway and set her down on a line of fishing pots and he told Kel payment of any kind would not be necessary.

'But she's from the towers,' said Kel. 'She's somebody.'

Kel knelt beside her friend and she told her to wake up, and when the man told Kel the girl wasn't nobody no more she shouted out the girl's name over to drown out all other noise and replace it with hope. When hope went it was replaced by rage, a fire that lifted her off her feet and dumped her burnt, busted and bruised and back where she belonged, alone.

She lay where she had fallen, and when they carried Rose away she let them, and she let the woman that was the man's wife take the baby toward the promise of warmth and shelter. Occasionally a lamp grew wide with cylindrical light as it swung her way and in her mind she told the couple that she would come in from the storm soon, but in reality she was mute to sense and she barely felt them load blankets upon her, and when the tide rose and came clawing at her feet she let them carry her inside because she knew those claws belonged to the island sea spirits come to pull her back in.

For what seemed like forever Kel lay mute and unmoving in a stranger's bed. The baby gone from her and Rose gone from the world complete. She could hear the clock on the bedside cabinet, its constant ticking a reminder that life went on, kept moving, but to Kel the sound was like a bomb waiting to go off.

She listened to the noise of the family and occasionally the baby cried, and each time he did a little of her came back to knowing that he cried out for her.

He called to her day and night and it was as if he were putting pieces of her back together bit by bit, but some days were better than others. The hounding ocean spirits had gone, but occasionally through the daze she imagined Rose standing at the bottom of the bed; there were times when the girl came closer, bent to kiss her, her hands in Kel's and her beautiful calm eyes smiling, all all right. Other people came too, the strangers from the beach, and she asked to see baby Rosen but they never answered her and soup was all they had to offer.

Days, nights, light coming through the curtain and then darkness. Kel spent her time eating and sleeping, getting stronger. Her only pleasure, the one thing she looked forward to, was buried in her imagination; Rose's spirit visiting each night, telling her to hurry up and get better, for the baby, for their future. Some nights Rose stayed and they were the best of nights, when she lay beside her and held her close, but in the morning Kel found the space next to her gone cold and the girl consigned to memory, just a fantasy moment. It was those times when Kel thought of all the things she should have said and all the things she would never say. It was love, but it went deeper than love; it was colour when she had never known colour, it was music when she had only ever known one tune. She thought about Rose's voice, the song she had sung that first day in the dinghy and it made her smile, made her cry.

The things that should have picked her up pushed her further into the bed, the clock ticking, the curtains opening and closing, until finally one morning a sound, faint at first, the tiny gurgle of a baby waking from his sleep; her baby.

Kel sat up and stretched from the bed. She stood at the window and opened the curtains and waited for the blood to reach her head, her legs weak, but in her heart a new kind of strength building bit by bit.

She dressed quietly and found her bag and slowly crept through the strangers' cottage. She was grateful for all they had done but if she woke them she would have to explain why she needed to get away, how there was nothing there for her, the baby was all she needed.

She found Rosen behind a closed door and when she picked him up he smiled and Kel smiled too. 'Just this,' she whispered. It was Rose who had helped her appreciate all that the baby was, good from bad. Kel told herself she would always make the best of things, always, for Rose.

When she was sure nobody was about she strode out into the dark-drawn day with the baby tied into the carrying thing she'd fashioned whilst on the island.

She walked into a new dawn storm. It stood steady behind her and pushed her forward through a maze of wet fields and busted boards, and she kept her mind clear of thinking, let the wind guide her toward higher ground.

Through the gusting rattle-run racket she didn't hear her name get called and she turned her head into her collar to keep the air out of her ears and then she pulled the blanket that covered the baby's head over her own the same. It was into this snood that she hid from the world except to keep step and footing.

'Kel!'

She could hear her name riding clear on the breeze and she recognised it as Rose's voice and she told herself that the girl was dead. No good came from want, no matter how it hurt to know this. And so she went on, definite in motion until the hand on her arm pulled her backwards.

'Kel,' shouted Rose and she held her almost to shaking until Kel returned her name.

'I thought you was dead,' said Kel. 'You was dead.'

Rose shook her head. 'I'm getting better.' She stood back to stick out her leg.

'You got a cast,' said Kel, stunned.

'Kind of. More of a splint really. That lady did it, she used to be a doctor. Why did you think I was dead?'

'That bloke. I said you had to be looked after cus you was tower folk and he said you werent nobody no more.'

'The *towers* are no more. They've been taken down, all the swampers rose up.'

'What about your lot?'

'Who cares? We did it, Kel. We're free.'

Both girls stood with the awkwardness of circumstantial intimacy between them and Kel said something about being glad that Rose hadn't died.

'Ha, so am I.' Rose smiled, and so did Kel.

'You stayin on with them olds?' she asked.

'Why?'

Kel shrugged. 'Maybe whilst you're still healin or whatever.'

'What about you? You've been sick these past days.'

'I have?'

Rose nodded.

'Might just go on now I'm headin.'

Rose nodded and Kel knew she was waiting for her to speak.

'I int so good with words,' said Kel and she wanted to scream all the love from her in one go.

'I know that.'

'But if you want to ...'

'Go on ...'

'You can come with me. Just if you want to, till you find somethin better or whatever.'

Rose started to laugh.

'What?'

'You've got no idea, Kel Crow.'

'Bout what?'

Rose smiled and took her hand and Kel noticed the tiny buds of colour on Rose's nails, pink.

'About love.' Rose wrapped her arms around her and told Kel she had missed her more than she'd ever thought possible. 'I even miss this bloody baby.' She bent to kiss Rosen.

Kel looked down at the ground; she wanted to tell Rose that she loved her so much that it was a new thing for her heart to contend with, that she loved her more than anything in the world.

'Rose?'

The girl nodded. 'I know.'

'You do?'

'Day one.'

'No, not day one.'

'Ha, I think so. I think you were in love with me the moment you saw me and saved me from the ship's crew.'

'That int how it went.'

Rose smiled. 'Whatever. So are you going to tell me the plan now?'

It was then that Kel realised for the first time that she no longer needed a plan. She put her hand to the heart that had broken and fixed itself right through compassionate and she promised herself that she would not set upon any course other than the one she was on. She had hope, and it was bigger than the swamps and bigger than the towers and bigger than the world she hated but would learn to love, and it was with that thought that she smiled suddenly. Kel Crow had survived, and she could now survive anything.

'Well?' Rose said again. 'Where we heading?'

'As far from the ocean as we can get,' said Kel.

Rose nodded. 'That sounds like just about the best plan I ever heard.'

She took hold of Kel's hand, and together they went on toward the new dawn rising.

About the Author

Natasha Carthew is a working-class country writer from Cornwall, where she lives with her girlfriend. She has written all her books outside, either in the fields and woodland that surround her home or in the cabin that she built from scrap wood. She has written two books of poetry, as well as three novels for young adults, *Winter Damage*, *The Light That Gets Lost* and *Only the Ocean*, all for Bloomsbury. Her first novel for adults, *All Rivers Run Free*, is published by riverrun/ Quercus. Natasha has written for many publications on the subject of wild writing, including the *Writers' & Artists' Yearbook*, Eco-fiction, TripFiction, the *Guardian*, the *Big Issue* and the Dark Mountain Project. She's currently writing her second literary novel for adults and a new collection of rural poetry.

Discover more from Natasha Carthew

BLOOMSBURY

Natasha
Carthew
winter
damage

'Elegantly lyrical'
Susan Elkin, *Independent*

'Gripping stuff . . . Carthew's prose has a startling ferocity'
Telegraph

The LIGHT THAT GETS LOST

NATASHA CARTHEW

BLOOMSBURY

'A wild and dangerous story and a beautiful one too'
The Bookbag